FATIMATA

FATIMATA

A Novel by Didier Périès

Translated by the DV Translation Group

Deux Voiliers Publishing
Gatineau, Quebec, 2025

Fatimata @ Didier Périès
Deux Voiliers Publishing
Gatineau, Quebec
www.deuxvoilierspublishing.com

Original Title: *Guelta : du Sahel au rugby* by Didier Pèriès
Translation: The DV Translation Group
Editor: Ian Thomas Shaw
Page Design, Cover Art and Layout: Ian Thomas Shaw

LIBRARY AND ARCHIVES CANADA CATALOGUING IN PUBLICATION

Title: Fatimata / a novel by Didier Périès ; translated by the DV
Translation Group.
Other titles: Guelta. English
Names: Pèriès, Didier, author.
Description: Translation of: Guelta: du Sahel au rugby. | In English,
translated from the French.
Identifiers: Canadiana 20250275570 | ISBN 9781928049616
(softcover)
Subjects: LCGFT: Novels.
Classification: LCC PS8631.E7336 G8413 2025 | DDC jC843/.6—
dc23

To

Erin, Ambroisine, Béni, Axel et Mattéo

—Generation Hope

We are not born strong, weak, or determined.
We become strong, we become clear-sighted.
— Meursault, The Stranger, Albert Camus, 1942

I am a force that moves.
                    — *Hernani*, Victor Hugo, 1829

HOW TO USE SPOTIFY

Open the white search bar at the bottom of your homepage; Tap on "What are you looking for?"; On the new screen, click the camera icon at the top right; Choose "scan" and aim your phone at the code above. NOW YOU CAN DIVE INTO THE WORLD OF FATIMATA

To my parents, on two continents.

To my grandparents, whom I never saw again.

To my beloved Abou and Amel,

who are with me every second of my life,

Nana

MONTAUBAN, SATURDAY, JUNE 22, 2024

FINAL OF THE REGIONAL JUNIOR WOMEN'S FIFTEEN RUGBY CHAMPIONSHIP

The sky celebrated the final by weeping with joy. My face was drenched. A stream poured down from my short, tightly braided hair across my eyebrows, down my cheekbones, flooding over my lips and dripping from my chin onto the pitch, green as a dream. Rather than wipe it away, I embraced the downpour. Unlike my teammates, who grumbled, I saw it as a sign of fate. That's why I had a little smile tugging at the corner of my lips, one I tried to hide. I was simply happy. In my mind, the first notes of a Youssou N'Dour song rose up. Everything was about to unfold in just a few seconds—and I intended to savour each one as if it were my last.

The downpour intensified. A moving curtain of rain blurred my view, but I could still make out the dark, dense mass of spectators packed into the grandstands on my right. Some thirty metres ahead, my gaze fixed on Lucie, our fierce little scrum-half. I saw her plant her cleated boot in a narrow gap amid the mess of limbs sprawled on the ground in front of her. She widened the breach with a yell—"Ruck! Ruck over!"—crouched low, pushing with her arms against the tangle of bodies. Then she plunged both hands into the gaping hole. With a sharp movement, she pulled out the drenched oval ball, which rolled at her feet.

She glanced back at us—the three other backs... and me. Then she called out: "At 45! At 45!" We all adjusted our positions. It was perfect in terms of depth. We were shaking from head to toe. From cold and from adrenaline. A powerful shiver shot down my spine. My left leg—my support leg—was bent, like a middle-distance runner on the starting blocks. I was ready. Ready for one more sprint.

We had already launched twenty attacks since the start of the game. The forwards had tried everything: pick-and-go, driving mauls, scrums. We, the backs, had been thrown in as a last resort. The team spread the ball wide, and we ran like crazy. Kicks over the top, grubbers, desperate passing sequences—cross passes, skip passes. And twenty times, we were stopped. The ball had only reached me once, off a desperate, sloppy pass from the inside centre. It was awful—a real floater.

One half spent gaining ground, a little, and losing it, a lot—dropping too many balls. Forty minutes mostly defending, but our defensive wall had held! Our opponents managed just one unconverted try. Not bad. And the whole second half, we were camped in their territory, laying siege to their try line. Not great. For thirty-five minutes, our world boiled down to two miserable digits: 5–0, blinking on the municipal field's scoreboard. That was still the score, just minutes from the end. The promised land still felt far away. Yet I'd never felt more ready than I did today. And it was raining for me.

Lucie, with one hand still on the ball at her feet, faked a pass. Her opposite number nearly dove over the offside line, risking a penalty, but backed off at the last second. "Gamma! Gamma!" Alexandra, our fly-half, called the play. The ref signaled for the ball to be played. The action kicked off in a flash. All the backs started running in unison. My heart leaped. A flood of adrenaline rushed through my entire body, to the tips of my fingers. I stared ahead, relying on peripheral vision for the rest.

I saw Lucie pass the ball to Alexandra with that characteristic dive of scrum-halves. The play was fully underway. I was overtaken by a wave of indescribable sensations, lost in the shouting of the players and the roar of the crowd. The oval ball continued its journey from hand to hand, getting closer. Just ahead of me, Caro—the same inside centre who had held onto the ball too long in the first half—managed to break through a gap between two players. I was flanking her, deliberately keeping a few metres behind. "I'm here, on the right, right!" As she reached the defender, she sidestepped, threw her opponent off balance, and, this time, sent me a perfect pass in stride, just as I was tearing forward like a rocket. Now it was my turn. I saw the open space in front of me and sprinted at full speed. I was in a trance. I ran like I had rarely run in my life. I was running on the sandy, stony tracks of my native Mauritania, running to save my brother, to save Abou, to survive. I was running to reach the *guelta*. I was running as if all our lives depended on it.

I was at the twenty-two metre line when I saw the powerful fullback charging down as the last line of defence. She was joining the winger who was already running toward me. Now I had only about a ten-metre corridor left. No time to think. I charged straight at the latter, taking a slightly angled trajectory: I had to move away from the touchline—a simple shove from her could push me out of play. She wouldn't even need to tackle me.

A heartbeat before contact, I shifted all my weight onto my left leg and made a deadly sidestep, extending my left arm to fend her off. She barely grabbed a piece of my jersey. I lifted my knee higher, twisted my hips, and shook free. She dropped, skidding into the turf. Five metres to go. I had one goal: to ground the ball behind the try line. Even touching the line would count. Without looking to my left—where I knew the fullback was closing in—I instinctively faked a torero move, hips swaying right. I was almost there…

Then I was grabbed and lifted off the ground in a tackle so violent it knocked the breath out of me. I was literally flying toward the touchline, my upper body still twisted left, stretching for the sacred line. "Don't drop the ball, don't drop the ball, relax…" I mentally hurled all my weight back infield, even knowing it might be useless. The ball, still miraculously clutched to my chest, I extended my right arm and grounded it —cleanly—in the corner!

I fell like an old, deflated ball into the corner of the field with a big "phew!", not quite sure if all or part of my body had gone out of bounds. That's what we French rugby players call *prendre un bouchon*—getting jammed hard near the sideline! But I was still alive and in one piece. Then I distinctly heard the referee's whistle. She wasn't far, somewhere ahead of me, probably with one hand raised, the other to her mouth holding the whistle. "Try awarded." With my nose pressed into the wet earth and freshly mown, water-soaked grass, I was dazed. I swallowed hard; my saliva tasted like blood. I felt like I was on a canoe in the middle of the ocean, suspended between the sky and the abyssal depths. I was about to faint. My muscles relaxed, and I felt myself slipping away. A strange thought came to me: I had finally reached my goal. It was the end of an Odyssey that had begun nineteen months earlier. And then a redemption as long as a child's wait before entering the world. A redemption that had started last August...

TOULOUSE, TUESDAY, AUGUST 15, 2023

Today, I'm starting my diary. My name is Nana, and it's my birthday. Marie gave me a notebook with blank pages and a lovely fountain pen with a red wooden cap and said, "It's a good time to start writing." Strangely, my heart started racing, and I suddenly felt an overwhelming urge to write something down. Out of politeness, however, I shook my head and said that I didn't know how to write very well in French.

"That's not true at all," Marie replied. "You're doing really well. You've clearly worked hard throughout your recovery. And even if there are a few mistakes, it doesn't matter, Nana. Nobody's perfect, and a diary isn't a writing contest! Remember what the psychologist said. It'll help you manage your emotions better, and maybe even bring back your memory."

"And you only become a writer by writing," added Santi, her husband, in an encouraging tone. "Don't worry about the mistakes!"

Marie went on to say that the avenue we live on is named after the founder of a literary prize that's awarded to books about Toulouse, its region, and its history, and that maybe it wasn't a coincidence that I was here, fountain pen in hand, holding this diary. I thought maybe, one day, I might be the one receiving an award from the Académie des Jeux Floraux (just that name makes me dream—it's so full of poetry). I felt more confident, stronger, and I smiled.

It's my first birthday here, even though I'm not sure of my real birth date. Everything is still so hazy in my memory. I don't even know what day, what month, or what year I was born! The doctors called it "trauma-induced amnesia." In Mauritania, I don't think we really celebrated birthdays, at least, not like this. What I do know is that I was born in the middle of the African winter, during the rainy season. So Marie, Santi, and I decided that my birthday would be August 15. According to our guesswork, that would make me sixteen.

Of course, it's just pretend. I didn't have any ID or passport when I was rescued, which didn't help. But really, what did it matter? When they questioned me after I woke up, I couldn't give them any information. I had forgotten everything. And even if I hadn't, I was far too scared. I couldn't, and wouldn't, say anything, not when they found me, adrift on my little piece of wood in the middle of the Mediterranean. Dehydrated, starving, "at death's door," as Santi says. He loves his metaphors. Still, they quickly figured out I was a girl, despite my short hair and how thin I was. They didn't even know who I had been travelling with, so they just made their own assumptions. I was too exhausted, too shell-shocked to explain more. I was like the living dead—alive, but not really.

In the end, the authorities treated me like any other refugee. What could I say to that? Reaching this point had been my deepest wish—I was sure of it, even if I barely remembered anything. But for Santi and Marie, I was more than just another refugee. At least, that's what they've told me more than once. Eventually, they brought me back with them to mainland Europe, since they were working with UNHCR. Then to their home country, France. And finally, into their home. They quite literally saved my life.

Maybe it was because the first words I said were in French. They say that in the water, half-dead, I was humming unintelligible phrases. That's what Santi said. Marie didn't add anything, but she was there too, so she knew. But it was Santi who pulled me aboard the rescue boat. After that, they didn't want to leave me. They wanted to take care of me like their own child. As if I had no family, no friends. Is that possible? A few months ago, I would've said it was destiny.

But this morning, something changed: I had a flashback. I was listening to the radio, and hazy images started to surface in my mind. I wasn't alone on that journey—Abou was with me. Abou, the one I sang songs with. Even when our Zodiac capsized. Suddenly, I was sure: the song I'd been humming when I was rescued was from the radio. Maybe I'd seen the music video before. We used to sing out the chorus again and again to keep our spirits up, to survive. Abou isn't dead—I'm sure of it. But where is he? No one knows. Did he make it to the mainland? Italy? That was our dream. Maybe he made it, though I've been told he's still missing.

I was lucky. There's no other explanation. I thought about it a lot in my hospital bed over those long months of recovery. That's why I no longer believe in God, at least for now. All I believe in is luck, blind chance. After several hospital visits, Santi and Marie sorted out the paperwork. I didn't ask about the details. I only know I spent three months in a UNHCR hospital. I was in no condition to be moved. I was injured, severely underweight, and ill. Medical tests diagnosed early-stage tuberculosis, along with exhaustion and post-traumatic stress. That, or something like it. I didn't feel different from anyone else. I thought about all the others who died, even if I couldn't remember their faces or names. I quickly shoved the memories of the shipwreck into a dark corner of my mind. It was the past, a past I preferred to forget.

Oh yes, they quickly realized I was underage. So I was placed in a special unit for children. I wasn't going to complain.

10

Santi and Marie. There's so much to say about them. They work for the UN—he's a logistician (a word that is still a mystery to me); she's a doctor with her own clinic. They came to visit me at the hospital every week. They called it a "follow-up." I thought they were just doing their jobs. It was kind of them. I barely spoke, just a word here and there. I was wary. I'd learned it was better to always respond in French, even if I saw in their eyes that they sometimes had to make an effort to understand. My accent, my lack of vocabulary, and my broken sentences—I realize that now.

After that, I spent three more months in a place with baths and saunas, at a sanatorium where they treated my tuberculosis. And again, they came every Saturday morning. From the beginning, Marie had said, "Your TB is in the early stages. You'll get through it. We'll help you with everything, Sweetheart."

Strangely, it's the end of that sentence that stuck with me: "*Sweetheart.*" It had been so long since anyone had called me that. It warmed my heart. I had to take a lot of medication—many pills that could've damaged my liver. But I got through it. I was stronger than I looked.

Later, one day, Santi added, "When you're discharged at the end of July, you'll come with us, if you're okay with that. We'd like to offer you a new home and a new life."

It was. I wanted to forget my past, to start over. So Santi and Marie became my new family. Before leaving the hospital room, I clearly remember stopping and turning my head. I had an idea—I don't know why—but I felt like I had to say it. I pointed to a calendar on the wall, the one with cats on it. I picked a random day in August.

"That's my birthday!"

And so, today I'm celebrating my first birthday here, in Toulouse, in France. I'm happy, even though thinking about Abou makes me sad. It's the first time that memories have come back with this much detail. At the same time, it feels like it's not really me. It's hard to believe—but it can't be false. How do I make sense of it? I decide to let it go, for now. I'll see what comes next.

Santi and Marie are amazing—with their love and their incredible gifts! In addition to the diary and the fountain pen, they gave me a cell phone! The first thing I thought when I held that little device in my hand: music! Now I can listen to music anywhere, anytime. I'll also be able to stay in touch with all my future friends from high school. But mostly, the music: I know how to find it, how to download it. With Santi and Marie's help, I did my first search—I typed in "birthday music." Result: we listened repeatedly to "Happy Birthday" throughout the meal! And we all cried. That's when Abou returned—fully. Abou, and all the others who were with us on the Zodiac.

Before the crossing? From her previous life, there is nothing. Just an immense, terrifying void. But her first memory from that time, after their first failed attempt, can be said in one word: Abou.

Abou and her, clinging to each other. Abou with his funny accent. Abou humming *On ira* by Zaz to comfort her. They were both crying. She was dazed. She remembered crying the whole way back to Nouadhibou, then all the way to the transit camp. People called it "Guantanamito."

Abou, though, kept humming Zaz's song, their only comfort. Fortunately, they were children, and looked like children. Luckily, her hips hadn't filled out yet. And together, their ages were barely thirty.

After two months in the camp, she was released, along with Abou, who claimed to be her brother, despite their slightly different skin tones. Who wasn't mixed, anyway? Since they had no documents to say otherwise, they were believed.

She left the camp with short hair, tiny dreads. It was more practical that way—no need to wash, less chance of lice. She also got used to flattening her budding chest with a strip of cloth. It spared her certain conversations. Instead of a headscarf, she wore a cap from then on. No gender trouble. No religious questions either.

That was also the last time she could send news to her parents. She had brought them shame. It was too late to turn back. And she didn't want to. But they had to know she was alive. Abou's friend's cousin, the teacher, had promised to deliver a message to them.

She had managed to keep her jewellery. She wanted to do her part, to pay Abou's way to Libya. They had been told: that's how the others made it to Europe. Italy, the new paradise.

The weeks slipped by. More screaming. She couldn't stand the screaming anymore, even though she'd been yelled at before. Now it was constant. Beggars in the street. Police chasing them. Smugglers barking at them like dogs. And each time, they had to pay, one way or another.

The smuggler for Libya took all her remaining jewellery. Then one morning, in the middle of the Algerian desert, he vanished.

By some miracle, there were no bandits, no police. It was easier to go unnoticed as a pair. She and Abou walked for days. They had become true travellers. They had time to talk.

She told him her story. He told her his: the eighth child, given over by his parents to a *marabout*. He was then eleven, had even been to school. But this was a *daara*, a Qur'anic school. He became a *talibé*.

"To eat there, you had to pay. To sleep, you had to pay. Even to learn the verses of the Qur'an, you paid. And they beat you with sticks."

So, he learned to beg. Learned to survive. And he got tired of it. He dreamed of more. Much more. Staring out at the ocean for hours.

Abou spoke Arabic, French, Wolof, Serer, and broken English. He taught her a few words—the most useful: *help, traveller, no papers.* And they sang to keep their spirits up. Sometimes they even danced, when the exhaustion didn't crush them.

They finally arrived somewhere: parched, covered in dust, indistinguishable from the land itself—Tamanrasset.

They quickly found work. No passport needed here. They washed dishes in a restaurant. But to go farther, they needed more money.

15

She thought of her parents. They were right—tourism paid. Three months' wages in Algerian dinars, plus a few dozen dollars for small services to tourists. Being cheerful, having a pretty smile, it all helped. Even if the bosses kept yelling, again and again.

For Libya, they didn't repeat the same mistake. It made Abou laugh. "We'll do it without a smuggler!" he kept saying.

So one day, they crossed the border. There was no line, no wall, no fence—just desert. The sand looked the same on both sides. It was a long walk, but they were used to walking.

Eventually, a sign riddled with bullet holes: Libya.

Avoiding Libyan detention camps was a miracle. In Algeria, they'd heard what Libyans did to migrants—regardless of skin colour, gender, or religion. Everyone talked. Everyone knew. Rape. Theft. Beatings. Torture. Caging. Like animals, or worse, like merchandise. Because animals fight back. Migrants, when worn down, don't. They just suffer. In silence.

Along the way, they met survivors. Sometimes. Poor souls heading back. But they kept going. Or searched for another route. Egypt? Maybe. But she and Abou didn't want to take detours. They wanted to reach their goal. Straight ahead. Risk be damned.

They were impatient and patient at once. But that wasn't the main thing.

At night, her little brother came to her in dreams. He screamed. And fell. Behind her, Mohamed Ould Obeid grabbed her. Touched her. She recognized the acrid smell of his sweat. Then he threw her from the battlements. She too was falling.

Always the same nightmare.

She woke with a jolt, wide-eyed. What if the Libyan police caught her? Or smugglers? The thought haunted her.

She barely slept. Ate little—roots, rice, dried fruit, rarely meat. She thought of the *Guetna* celebration. Juicy dates.

She'd lost more weight. But her body was changing. Her breasts were growing. Abou didn't seem to notice.

Weeks of arid wandering and shared hardship passed. They reached the coast, near Tripoli. Now they had to find a boat. Abou wasn't laughing anymore.

But first, a smuggler. Easy enough to find, but tricky to trust. Was he honest? Was he lying? How could they know? Abou tried to reassure her: "It's like Russian roulette," he said. She didn't understand, but smiled anyway.

They handed over all their savings to the smuggler, who shouted when he spoke.

"We're not deaf!" she wanted to scream. She couldn't take it anymore. But she said nothing.

Now they truly had nothing left. Their last hope. Too proud to show it. She could still pass as a boy—despite her wider hips.

A boat would leave in two nights. Safe passage, they were told. Drinking water for three days. *Inshaa Allah*. She repeated the words. She wanted to believe them.

The smuggler hadn't laughed. That gave her hope. But she didn't dare ask the question that terrified her: How many passengers? What kind of boat? Abou was silent too. Despair was near. But so was Europe.

A few days later, they were hidden among rocks, on the edge of the sea. It seemed as vast as the ocean. Their new home under open sky.

They ate seaweed and little crabs, waiting for the smuggler's signal. Over a hundred people were hidden on the wet sand.

She had nothing else to do. She stared at her arms. Veins bulging. Where had her smooth, full skin gone? Cracked. Burned. Filthy.

Abou's hand could wrap around her wrist now.

Her final memories of that time remain vivid.

She was on the water—this time, the Mediterranean. Unbelievable to say. Even more so to live. The swell. The seasickness—again. But she was used to it now.

At first, they still sang—songs heard on Algerian radio. *travellers,* by K-Iri. To keep their spirits up. But soon, groans and sobs replaced the music. And filth mixed with seawater at their feet.

They were crammed too tightly to move. Her legs were numb. Around fifty desperate people. Among them, women and children. It changed nothing. There was still no land in sight. The sun scorched them by day. At night, cold spray chilled them. Waves could toss them overboard. Or a fellow passenger could. One fewer person to drink the boat's supply of water. So, she and Abou took turns sleeping. They barely spoke. They didn't sing anymore.

One time, he whispered, looking at her: "There's something dancing inside you." A declaration of love? Delirium? The last words she remembers. Then nothing. Had she even remained conscious? Hard to say.

After three days, no more water. The smuggler had been right. The days stretched out—ten, perhaps twelve? They drank urine. Drank seawater. Lips caked in salt. She lost all sense of time. Of other people.

She kept her eyes on Abou. He was her anchor.

Only Abou mattered. And—absurdly—the floating logo of France 24, shimmering in the air.

In her mind, they still sang. Still danced to *On ira*. She was hallucinating. Or dreaming with open eyes.

Then, suddenly, she was in the water. Ears, nose, mouth flooded. She swallowed gulps of salt water. She couldn't swim! Panic. She looked around. Everyone was screaming. Children cried—briefly—then fell silent.

The Zodiac was collapsing. Sinking.

Some tried to climb back on.

She didn't see Abou.

Her arms ached. She searched for him.

Now it was her turn to scream—again and again. She forgot her body, the muscle pain. She thrashed, calling his name.

She had forgotten she couldn't swim. Then remembered. Panic again.

Her body remembered: Abou had taught her how to tread water. She closed her eyes. Murky water engulfed her.

A memory of an oasis. Smooth water soothing her muscles.

No one moved around her anymore. They were all gone. Abou was gone. She would never see him again. And yet—no tears came. Had she gone too?

Then, she saw a piece of the boat. A broken plank. A bench slat. Big enough to hold her weight. She was at her limit. One last effort. She hoisted herself onto the wood.

In the end—yes to life. No to death.

"A decent, stable life. You're entitled to one, my little darling." Marie loves calling me that—*choupinette*. It still sounds strange, especially the first time I heard it at the hospital, a few months ago. Part of me liked it. Another part... questioned it. What gave her the right to use such tender words? Deep down, at first, a small voice whispered: *Too nice to be sincere.* But I shut the voice down. I liked it when she used those affectionate nicknames.

"Nana" worked too. Nana reminded me of Mauritania, but not in a bad way. It depended on who was saying it, the tone, the situation. I carried those memories of months of wandering and the shipwreck...

But a "decent, stable life"? That was funny! Yes, really—a funny idea. Since it was new to me, I tried to understand, but didn't really succeed. So I looked at her with wide eyes. Two heads shorter than her husband, a beautiful woman with curvy hips and rectangular glasses that made her look serious, even when she laughed. Her dark eyes were slightly almond-shaped, her cheekbones high, and her coppery skin much lighter than mine. Her skin looked silky—you wanted to reach out and touch it. The morning sun lit her up so much it almost blinded me. I blinked. She went on:

"It's been eight months today since we met. I know it's an anniversary you'd rather forget, but are you aware of how far you've come? You've put back on some weight and filled out. I'm almost certain you've even grown a few centimetres. You can see the top of my head now, can't you? And not to mention your progress at school. Your French is so much better—as good as any kid you'll meet there. And you'll be back in school soon, in high school! We're so proud of you."

I lowered my head. I could feel myself blushing. Compliments make me uncomfortable. Do I deserve them? I feel like I still struggle with long sentences, expressions, or some verb tenses. So I prefer silence. Marie doesn't seem to mind—she goes on.

"With that funny little voice of yours, do you realize there's something special inside you? I see it. And so does Santi. Do you even realize the strength and courage you've shown?"

"Luck, mostly."

"Maybe. But don't put yourself down. It's more than that. A little extra soul! That's it! Like your powers are still asleep

22

inside you. Others will see it too. Anyway, thank goodness for TV, the internet, and distance learning! You're missing only one thing, maybe. Don't you miss running? Doing sports? You said you remembered liking physical activity in Mauritania. That was a long time ago, but still..."

"Okay, is there a running club here?"

"Yes. But no, I was thinking of something else where you would run a lot too."

I had played hide and seek with the neighbours' kids, but I was too old for that now. I also played soccer with them—I liked it, it was fun—but I didn't dare shoulder-check anyone. It was like I was afraid. Afraid of them? Of hurting someone? What was happening to me? Back in Mauritania, I was the one who wouldn't hold back.

Marie was hiding something. She wanted me to guess. We played that game a lot. It helped me learn many new words. She wanted me to ask a question.

"Is it a sport where you run?"

I already knew the answer, but it was a good place to start.

"Yes."

"Do you do it alone?"

"No."

"In pairs?"

"No."

"In groups?"

"Yes."

"Do you need equipment?"

"Yes... but not much."

"Okay. I think I've got it. Is it a ball sport?"

"Yes, you're almost there…"

"Soccer?"

"No."

"Hmm."

"Come on, try again!"

"Volleyball? Handball? Basketball?"

"No, no, and no."

At that point, I was stumped. I searched hard—I saw images in my mind. The oldest ones, the newest—I mean, the ones that were coming back to me, from less than two years ago. TV, internet, YouTube, World Cup, Olympic Games… Santi had shown me so many different sports too. Here, people do so many activities, with all kinds of gear. They call it *leisure*, because they have time—or they make time for it.

Which one to choose, among all he'd shown me?

"Is it underwater?"

I was thinking of underwater hockey, but I didn't say it.

"No."

"I'm stumbled."

"Stumped. Stumbled is when you fall. Stumped is when you can't figure it out."

"Okay. Will you tell me the answer?"

"No."

Seeing my stunned face—stunned, I love that word—she laughed loudly.

"I'll do better. To celebrate our eight-month anniversary, we're going to get the answer in person. Do you trust me? Throw something on! We're going out."

A year ago, I wouldn't have answered. Or I would have hesitated, afraid of making a mistake and getting sent away. No one knew where I came from. Most people guessed Central Africa. With my dark skin, full lips, high cheekbones, and frizzy hair... The Congo? Or farther east, Sudan?

Me, I had long known, without really knowing why, that I was Mauritanian. To most people, I looked like a refugee. That was as far as it went.

Every day, the TV news confirmed it. At first, that was all the entertainment I had. But every news report or drama show felt like going home, back to square one. But I didn't want that! How to explain it? When people asked me questions during my recovery, I stayed mostly silent. A few French words: yes, no, hello, goodbye.

Marie and Santi understood. They eventually gave up that battle. They took me as I was. That was enough. And I was happy—apart from the nightmares and nighttime panic attacks.

"The ghosts of the past live within us," Santi once said.

No. For me, they haunt us.

It scared me. That's why, in the beginning, I slept in their room, on a cot. Now I had my own room, but on nightmare nights, they came running immediately. They sat on my bed, comforted me, and Marie held me in her arms.

And then, one day, at the start of the month, I spoke. For real. I made sentences. With verbs.

It was the end of dinner. We were still all three at the table, with Mistigri the cat and Bobette the Swiss shepherd as witnesses. Nothing funny, nothing serious or special. I don't remember exactly—I think I wasn't even listening to the conversation. As often I did, I had drifted into a soft daydream. Then suddenly, I opened my mouth and told them everything— everything about the last weeks before the shipwreck.

Without stopping.

No one interrupted me as I poured it all out. I cried as I spoke. Marie and Santi cried too. The dog came and licked my hand.

In that precise moment, I understood that I was placing my life back into their hands. It wasn't planned, but something had clicked in my head. Despite the images that now filled my sleep more and more often, I suddenly trusted these two adults I barely knew.

Did my outpouring change anything? Hard to say. But I think they understand me better now. And for trust, things really did change.

"Let's go! I can't wait to see your surprise. Can I ask one more question?"

"You just did. You've used up your bonus questions."

"Huh?"

"Just kidding! Go ahead! There's no such thing as a bad question."

"Is it with boys and girls? I mean, is it mixed?"

"Mixed? No, except for very young children, boys play on their own. There are women's and men's teams."

"Is it played all over the world?"

"Yes. And now, Nana, that's two questions. So be patient. You'll see. And maybe you'll even get to try it out."

"I'd rather watch first."

I've always been that way, I think. I didn't feel completely at ease, but I was curious. And off we went.

As we left the driveway and turned onto Avenue Camille Pujol, I glanced at the house I'd now been living in for a month. Santi had explained that this kind of home is called a *Toulousaine*: attached to its neighbours, low-lying, originally single-storey, made of pink brick and river stones—*galets*— from the Garonne, the river that runs through Toulouse.

This type of house isn't very big, but Marie and Santi's has an upper floor for the bedrooms and a kitchen extension in the back with a bay window. That part opens onto a garden with grass, trees, and even flowers. There's also a small front garden with not much in it—they told me they don't have a "green thumb," which surprised me at first, until they explained the expression. Still, there's a little laneway to park the car.

They told me that in the past, the people who lived in these homes grew their own vegetables to sell at the Sunday markets in town. This was because the area used to be a *faubourg*, something between a suburb and the city.

It's all fenced in with a low wall.

Not far from the house, there's a sports complex near the beltway, in the Argoulets neighbourhood. There are outdoor playing fields, a running and walking track, and a big gymnasium. It's beautiful, and I'm always amazed at how green it is.

We'd walked there before. But this time, as soon as the car was parked, Marie got out quickly and headed straight ahead. She was going to a specific field.

I followed, obedient, quickening my pace. I lifted my head, squinted to see better. Two tall posts at each end of the field, with a crossbar. As long as a soccer field.

I understood—I had seen it on TV before. But never in real life.

Girls were already running across the field, an oval ball in hand.

Toulouse, Sunday, August 27, 2023

This afternoon, Santi and Marie introduced me to François. Sorry, Franck, that's what he prefers to be called. He arrived at the house completely drenched in sweat. It didn't really bother me—heat and sweat, I know them too well. Always have. And even more now that I remember what happened before I was rescued. Not that I'm happy about those memories—I hope they stay buried deep in the back of my mind.

In any case, Santi seemed a little reluctant to shake Franck's hand, who apologized, saying he had just run all the way to our place. Apparently, he's always running. Always on the move— from home to university, from university to work, to buy bread, to go play tennis. All the time. Hence the sweat. I kind of liked that. I also go jogging almost every day. And people have always told me I run fast.

But I was a bit surprised. He was the piano teacher? Shorts and a T-shirt, a cap half-backwards on his head, running shoes. Not exactly how I imagined a piano teacher would look like. But what would I know? I'd never actually met one! The only image that came to mind was Mozart—with his wig in total disarray, shaking his head like he was possessed by a demon! But not all pianists wear wigs!

Marie ran off to the laundry room and came back with a towel. Franck wiped himself down. His face was flushed and panting at first. Then we saw the young man with his delicate features, sharp black eyes, a thin mustache and a small goatee like a musketeer.

He introduced himself and said he was twenty-five. But he didn't look it. He was rather short, about 1.70 metres by my guess. I could look him in the eye without trouble. But he seemed a little skinny next to me—I'm curvier now. I still kept my head lowered. He was very friendly. He said he was studying mathematics, which, according to him, goes well with piano, maybe even gives him an edge. He explained that notes and rhythm, all of music theory, are based on math. Reading sheet music, counting beats, recognizing musical patterns—it all requires mathematical skills.

While he spoke, I noticed Santi nodding, glancing at me sideways. Yes, I got it too: learning piano would help me improve in math at school. He added with a scholarly air:

"And your coordination, Nana—which is already great from what I hear (wink at Marie)—will improve even more. That's important for rugby, right? Using both hands—cool, eh?"

"What do you think, sweetheart?" Marie chimed in. "We talked about you taking music lessons. You like music, and we wanted to give them to you as a present. Once you've got the music theory down, you can choose whatever instrument you like. It's a great foundation."

Of course, I agreed. Music is part of my life every hour of the day and night. It always was, and even more so now. Like a breath of oxygen that I need to avoid suffocating.

"Yes, I'd love to."

My heart was racing and overflowing with joy. Having a teacher just for me, just to learn music! I was already imagining playing guitar and drums. It stirred beautiful memories of Africa, even if they were hazy. Memories of sounds, of women drumming on goat-skin drums or on anything that could resonate, to celebrate. I wasn't starting from zero, really. But it all still felt locked away in my head. I was happy, but still not quite able to express it. So I smiled. I secretly hoped they understood.

Once introductions were done, we moved to the living room, where the upright piano stood proudly. An old piano from the early 20th century. Santi and Marie had bought it a few years ago—more for the decor, they said. It was rustic, like the rest of their furniture. They'd also been thinking of having a child one day, who could take lessons on it. In any case, the piano was already tuned—Santi had brought in a professional to do that.

Franck sat down on the bench as if he'd always belonged there. He began to play an upbeat jazz tune. Then he switched smoothly to some rock, before seamlessly ending with a classical piece. With stunning ease. I recognized those genres well enough to tell them apart, but not much more. The room was silent. I was speechless. Marie brought us back to reality.

"Have you had formal training?"

"Yes, at the conservatory. I stopped teaching there over the summer to give private lessons year-round. It pays better and the schedule's more flexible. I've completed all my levels. Besides that, I play in a band and I compose music. That's really my passion."

He spoke honestly, with no pretense, and in a relaxed tone. I immediately liked his attitude.

Clearly convinced, Santi continued:

"All right then. As I said on the phone, we're thinking one to two times a week. An hour each time. We also discussed the fees... But this is only if Nana agrees."

Marie looked at me. I murmured a barely audible yes.

"Okay, great. Would she like to start today?"

François turned to me with a smile. Same answer—I nodded timidly.

"Come on then, take the bench. I'll grab a chair. I've got one or two things to show you."

He started playing again—warm, enthusiastic.

"Know what this piece is called? *The Quiet Voice*. Like you. Beautiful, isn't it? You've got a funny little voice. I bet it's beautiful when you sing. That's a gift from above, you know? We'll sing together if you want."

His voice was a little raspy and youthful. It reassured me. I stepped closer.

And that's how I played my first piano improvisation, the very day I learned my first scale.

"Here, want to listen to a song for next week? Do you know Zaz? I'll play it... *On ira...*"

Zaz? That couldn't be a coincidence! And then I thought: he sings as well as he plays. Could Abou have played music like that? I will never know.

And my mind drifted, despite myself, far from here, farther south.

On ira...

CHINGUETTI, MAURITANIA – JUNE 2020

She's not the eldest, no. The eldest is a man. Well—a man... a seventeen-year-old boy. Her big brother. Maatallah.

When they were very little, they used to sleep in the same bed. Another warm body beside her on freezing nights. It felt good. He was affectionate. Then he began sleeping separately. He drifted away. Now he has hair on his face. He looks down on her. Talks to her like a father. He gives orders. Especially if she brings their little sister along to play. He doesn't joke anymore.

But he's the eldest. So for his wedding, the family goes all out. Her parents invite the whole extended family, who join the bride's family. Two days and two nights of celebration. As far as she can remember, she's never seen her family gathered like this. Nearly a hundred people. Several are still enslaved. They had to ask their masters for permission to attend.

Her grandparents rented out the Chinguetti community hall, in the new part of the city. That alone says it all.

After 10 p.m., the police start rounding up Black people, beating up some of them. So it's either pay a bribe or stay inside.

The first evening, greetings go on forever. Everyone asking about each other's health, work, home region... Years of news exchanged in minutes! Mint, or basil, tea is served. Several times. Amid incredible noise. The children are separated. Sent to bed quickly, so the adults can talk among themselves.

The next day begins with the ceremonies. After morning prayers. First, everyone gathers. With tea. Again.

The women in their *melafahs* and brightly coloured matching dresses. Kilos of jewellery—layered necklaces, bracelets, tiaras gleaming more brilliantly than the last. The men wear shimmering *drâas* in damask bazin, adorned with luxurious borders, over *sarouels* held up by finely tooled leather belts. Around their necks or heads, flowing white *halouis*.

They've set up tents as well. Just outside the town. Where the dunes begin to take over the streets.

The men on one side, the women on the other. With the children. They sit down. The floor is covered in brightly patterned mattresses and cushions. Chatter fills the air.

Some women pick up drums. Others grab a cooking pot. A chant rises, slowly. A rhythm, steady or not. One or two more talented women add their voices. Then everyone joins in, in chorus.

And then—they dance. Even the children. Giant platters of rice and chicken arrive. Mothers call out to their children in a kind of joyful chaos. Groups form again around the food. The tea is even sweeter now.

The *asr*, the third prayer of the day, approaches. The songs resume, between pauses where people nap. The children have already run off to play in the dunes.

As evening falls, a cooling breeze settles in. Soothes the spirit.

By 8 p.m., everyone returns. The hall fills again. It's the highlight of the evening. A famous traditional singer takes the mic. She climbs onto the large makeshift stage. Just some wooden planks and metal grating. A floodlight in each corner.

Then the dancers appear—with their slow, graceful movements. Each one in a different dominant colour. A whirling, multi-coloured ballet. *Youyous* ring out in celebration.

She finds herself crying out like the others.

The men aren't left out. They take to the stage in their *boubous*. Twisting, stretching, contracting. Moving to the beat. Everyone watches their feet most of all. Feet that launch them high into the air.

Her brother is honoured in front of them all. Maatallah, the prince of the day. He dances alone to the rhythm of the *redh*. She shouts louder when he leaps or twirls.

The fever dies down after about an hour. The final round of tea is served. The air is cooler now.

The bride and groom are finally allowed to see each other. But tonight, they leave separately.

Tomorrow will be more religious. The *medh* will dominate. And gifts will rain down. Before the farewell greetings. The whole family will make sure that everyone's stomach is full and the guests have enjoyed their three servings of tea before departing.

Zouerate, Nouadhibou, Nouakchott, Selibabi, Oualata. Names that make the young girl dream.

And her brother will leave home with his new wife.

But before that, there is the night.

There is the sharing of sleeping space.

Too many guests to fit in their home. Most sleep on the floor in the large hall. Others in the tents. Some at her cousins' places.

She lies down next to a cousin from the city—Aïcha. Same age, same height, but a different look in her eyes. Several times, she's caught Aïcha's amused glances. Slightly condescending. Well hidden, though. A discreet attitude.

She felt drawn to her. Wanted to talk to her. To touch her.

She finds her again in bed. There, they can whisper. Talk about anything. Aïcha tells her about life in the city. Parties with friends. Music. Alcohol. Boys. It's like being entrusted with her secrets. So thrilling!

Nearby, the younger children are sound asleep. After so much excitement, they dropped off the moment their heads hit the pillow.

Aïcha suggests a little game. Guessing the numbers she draws on her back. She lifts her nightgown. The two girls take turns letting their fingers wander across each other's skin. Time flows differently. Like an eternity. Like a slow caress. Sometimes the hands drift. It sends shivers all the way down to the belly.

"Nana, it's forbidden," Aïcha whispered tenderly.

She pulls her hand away. Returns to the back. And traces a three-digit number—harder to guess.

Time passes like that. The night deepens. She wishes it could last forever. But in the end, arms grow tired, and sleep overtakes them.

She will never see Aïcha again.

TOULOUSE, SEPTEMBER 4, 2023

First day of school! I really don't feel well—my heart is racing, my palms are sweaty. As I step outside the house, anxiety rises. I look around, my eyes drawn to countless details, but I can't see past the rows of houses and apartment buildings. I feel trapped, suffocated. The horizon suddenly seems sealed off. Something brushes my arm. I jump, then realize it's Marie's hand.

She's followed me out of the house, which is in an old neighbourhood called Guilheméry, named after an adventurous aviator from the early twentieth century. It's a place where trees have had time to grow, so there's a lot of shade, but the streets are narrow. Since we're at the top of a hill, you have to take the "Cobblestone Slope," a strange name since there are no cobblestones. You have to go down one side of the hill or the other before climbing again to go either to downtown or to the suburbs. I feel the calming pressure of her hand on my forearm as she walks me toward the car.

Marie and Santi insisted on driving me together. In the car, we always listen to the radio, which I like. And it's not always old stuff, because they have eclectic tastes, as Santi says. I love that word—it snaps off the tongue and I like what it means, too. So they switch radio stations depending on their mood, and I discover new singers, especially women singers. Like Fischer or Marwa Loud. This morning, it got me in the mood for high school. Or so I thought...

It's the big leagues now—at least that's what the tall, "lanky" guy (another funny word I try to remember!) who's become a second father to me, says. Santi always relishes adding something, just like a teacher. "You should be proud. All the distance learning you did these past few months has paid off! But be careful—that was just the first step, although an essential one. It doesn't mean things will be easy from here on out, okay? Don't hesitate to ask the adults. They're there to lend you a shoulder."

"To lend me *a shoulder* to cry on?"

"Almost. It just means 'to help you.' Like in rugby, in a scrum. Get it?"

"Somewhat. But I haven't tried rugby yet..."

"Okay, sweetheart. Santiago, don't mix her up with your idioms. Maybe this isn't the best time for a language lesson."

She leaned over to kiss me. I flinched a little, but managed not to pull away. Marie didn't react—she seemed not to notice.

"Anyway, don't be afraid. All the adults at school are ready to help you succeed. They explained that during your first visit, didn't they?"

"Yes."

"That said, you're going to get a lot of information all at once. You might feel a little... how should I say it? Buried under it all? That's normal. Don't panic. Don't expect to remember or understand everything right away. Give it time. Things will come together in a few weeks. Starting at a new school (and even more so in a new country, I thought to myself), it's never easy. For anyone. And besides, you won't be the only one. In *Seconde* (Grade Ten), everyone's new!"

"Okay."

I was left speechless after all that. I didn't get it all, but I felt a bit more reassured, even as my heart pounded harder the closer we got to the school. We had received material to prepare for the start of classes, after the tests I took earlier in the summer. I remember: math, French, history, geography, and life sciences. It was manageable—I'd done a bit of science before, and I'd been studying on the computer during my recovery these past few months. Math and French—I was okay. History and geography... that was new. So I'd tried to learn, and understand the whole curriculum at home. In three months! Apparently, I have an excellent memory. Luckily, Santi and

41

Marie supported me, but I had no one to compare myself to—I didn't have any friends my age yet.

The night before, I'd had that hollow feeling in my stomach —or more like a knot. It felt like I couldn't gather my thoughts. A kind of panic. Even thinking about the next day made my heart beat faster. In my mind, I'd just finished primary school. Flashes of memory returned—maybe the stress brought them back. They were quite clear, but I wasn't sure I wanted to share them with the psychologist. The happy memories often came bundled with sad ones from my old life, which didn't make me want to talk. I remembered the subjects we studied: Arabic as a first language, French as a second, drawing, a bit of physical education, some science, and the history and geography of Mauritania. That's how it was at twelve years old in Mauritania. What you would normally expect. But now I'm sixteen. And stepping back into a school was both exciting and strange.

I already knew a bit about the place because new students had been invited for a tour in early August—and we'd gone. A school with an actual campus had immediately impressed me. How could I imagine spending the next three years here? That meant not one building, but several, spread across kilometres. A stadium with grass and bleachers, a running track, and two indoor gyms. It made me dizzy. I hoped I'd be able to find my way easily between classes, right from the first day, and not end up lost somewhere. Or worse, be late for class, because I'd read that there were only five minutes between periods.

As soon as I reached the main building, I was "taken care of," as they say. Older students were welcoming new ones outside of it. I recognized a player from my rugby team—smaller than me, red hair, green eyes. She smiled at me and welcomed me. She said her name was Lucie, like the light. And she showed me about. I went to confirm my registration at a table with a nice man behind it. The school principal was there too, standing to the side with a warm smile and a kind word for each of us. Mostly to reassure the newcomers, I thought. But actually, she was also speaking to the others, shaking their hands too.

I was quickly directed to a corner of the large entrance hall, with big bay windows, toward a group of about ten students—all looking a bit bewildered, eyes slightly teary. Apparently, they came from more diverse backgrounds than the rest—Asian, Middle Eastern, African...

Marc and Jessica were there. My two teachers, whose first names I knew because they had taken the time to establish "personal contact" (that sounds so official!). A week earlier, I had spoken to them briefly via video call. So I was on familiar ground with them, and I felt reassured.

My class was a transition class, with fewer students, designed to bring us up to level to join a regular class the following year. This special class had only twelve students and two teachers who shared all the subjects. They even taught physical education together—co-ed. I was a little nervous and found that kind of unsettling: a sixteen-year-old boy can be pretty strong, right? In sports, what chance did a girl have against him? I reminded myself that I used to be just as fast as the boys at running. Then I thought about the locker rooms, where you had to change in front of everyone, but at least that part wasn't with the boys.

A few minutes later, they took attendance. It was kind of funny to see them try to pronounce all those foreign names. I tried not to smile so I wouldn't hurt their feelings—they were doing their best and correcting themselves after asking some students for the proper pronunciation of their names. Some students just smiled awkwardly while others scowled and repeated their name in a sharp, offended tone.

Then the teachers gave us our schedules and repeated that if our level in a subject improved enough during the school year, we would be sent to classes with the other students. Oh, and we were strongly encouraged to sign up for "cultural or sports activities," which I understood, sort of, but not really. I timidly raised my hand and asked for clarification. They explained these were clubs held during the long lunch break—nearly two hours! The goal was to help us integrate, they said.

And on top of that, we had our own classroom, the same one for all our courses (or almost—all except for science, the arts, and sports), and it was close to the cafeteria.

As soon as we got our schedule, I read and reread it carefully. Classes started at 8 a.m. and ended at 4 p.m.! I couldn't believe it! Even with a two-hour break, it was a long day, much longer than in Mauritania. I would have understood if it had been just until 2 p.m., but 4 pm? And every day, we had eight subjects in 45-minute periods. Eight different subjects, it was unimaginable! Even though I had read the information the school had sent over the summer, only now did I understand why people here seemed to know so much.

I even got to choose an elective (*biology and health*), and I was done with Arabic (phew!), but had to take English. And one course I was really excited to discover: culture and citizenship. I wanted to dive even deeper into this culture and not have to think about the past.

In arts, we'd study and practice a different discipline each trimester: visual arts, music, and performing arts. *Performing arts*? Theatre! I felt a wave of fear wash over me—I was nowhere near ready to be on stage in front of everyone!

The other big moment of the day was lunch. The cafeteria was a large, light-filled room surrounded by bay windows. We got there after the bell, along with hundreds of other students. There was already a long line to get a meal tray, and the noise level was overwhelming. I felt dizzy and instinctively covered my ears. On the bright side: the entire scene was bathed in radiant sunlight—it felt unreal.

I followed the crowd of students toward the serving line. After nine months, I'd had time to get used to the rich variety of food, so I wasn't surprised by the menu. Then it hit me—I could almost taste it, smell it—back in my school in Mauritania, we had only one meal option: rice or millet, Monday to Friday. Here, it was paradise, and now I had just one thought: taste everything.

Just as I was about to grab my starter, two people shoved past me in a blur. I didn't have time to see their faces. A boy and a girl—he was tall, messy hair, jeans. But her—I recognized her immediately. She was mixed-race, stocky, nose in the air, wearing Bermuda shorts and running shoes.

One or two people behind me grumbled a bit, but that was it. By the time I opened my mouth to protest, they had already grabbed their plates. And not a word—not even a glance from them!

A dark energy rose in me, and this time, I didn't have to force myself to speak.

"Hey, excuse me. You just cut in front of me. And there are tons of other students behind..."

My voice barely rose above the cafeteria noise, but at least I spoke, cold and firm. I spoke again, louder, trying to stay calm to give her one last chance. No response.

"Karen, don't you recognize me? It's Fatimata from rugby. If you'd asked, I might've let you in..."

"Oh, right. Didn't see you there, newbie! Tough luck!"

"Don't look at us like that," said the boy. "Trying to hex us like a *marabout*? With your witch hair, no wonder you're all alone..."

He towered over me, taller than Santi. A real "beanpole" (a weird word I got from Santi)! I was in shock. I looked around. My classmates from the transition class were behind me. People were staring, but no one stood up for me.

I felt a huge weight landing on my shoulders. I was paralyzed. My mind raced in circles. The noise around me seemed louder, the smells more intense. A chill ran down my spine.

I could have said something back, but what else could I have added?

Here, in just a few months, I'd already heard the word "racism" a lot. At least people said it out loud. I had sometimes noticed the stares, but never words this cruel. Racism was even a public topic, on TV, on the radio, on social media. Good! At least it was discussed.

I knew that in Mauritania, it was much worse. There, racism was so ingrained in people's minds that everyone practiced it— it didn't need to be spoken about. It was taboo, but present everywhere. Back there, I'd always lived with a clear idea in mind: a social hierarchy based on skin colour. At the top, the white Moors (*Beïdanes*), in the middle, Black Africans like the Peuls and many other ethnic groups and tribes. And then me— or rather, us—the Haratines, Black but Arabic-speaking.

What was worse? Being Haratine in Mauritania or being Black in France? Did they think they could traumatize me? Did I even want to answer them? In the end, I gave up. Karen had already turned away and was choosing her dessert.

I'd lost my appetite. I left the line without looking back and returned to my classroom.

I needed to let off steam this afternoon. I needed it to stop myself from thinking about memories from before, and about those few irritating details of life at school. Emma had confirmed it last week: since this was my third week of rugby, I'd start contact training. During the last two practices, I'd done more or less the same as the first, but we'd also added some touch rugby to start practicing real play. I loved it—running, passing, running again, and more running. My sprints had impressed everyone.

Already the days were getting shorter, the sun setting earlier. In the afternoons, it was cooler now, almost chilly in the shade of the trees. I felt it right away as I started walking down to the Argoulets. I'd learned that in Occitan, *argolets* meant kids, little children. I wanted to believe this place would become a kind of refuge, a space to distance myself from my worries. I had been there before, with Santi, or with Marie, or all three of us. We often walked Bobette there, enjoying the calm of the place, even though it bordered Toulouse's inner ring road.

There are so many facilities on these 43 hectares of green space! A metro station, a swimming pool, tennis courts, a cyclocross track, football and American football fields, walking and running trails, a judo dojo and martial arts gym. There's even a kind of meadow where I once saw sheep grazing. Though my memories are still hazy and incomplete, it reminds me most of the untouched nature I once knew. Actually, I've only ever known this type of "green zone" under the blazing heat of summer, when everything was more yellow than green —which might explain why I like it so much. In any case, it remains a haven of peace for me, under the trees planted more than forty years ago. It can even get a bit cold there, like it has recently, which is why I was wearing my club sweatshirt.

I put in my earbuds, chose a song with a good rhythm to get me going, and arrived a bit early. I preferred it that way to last-minute arrivals—it gave me time to prepare calmly and focus. I had already put on my shorts and team jersey at home, but not my socks or cleats. I liked walking in sandals—the lingering summer heat helped. I dropped my bag at the usual spot, a few metres from the sideline, near the bleachers.

Lucie arrived shortly after me, as cheerful and upbeat as ever, and came to stand next to me. She took off her cap, and her long curly hair fell onto her shoulders. A musky wave of scent filled my nostrils.

"So, Nana, how's your first week of school going?"

"Not bad, I'm getting used to it."

"Sorry, I haven't come to talk to you since the first day. I saw you a few times from a distance. I should've come over. You don't feel too lost, do you? Sometimes that happens to grade tens. Message me if it does."

"I'm lucky—I'm in the same class for half my courses so far."

"Okay, great. You ready for contact today? Remember: technique matters more than strength when you start. You'll have plenty of time to show off your power."

I didn't get the joke at first. Suddenly, I felt embarrassed.

"I... I..."

I quickly looked around to see if anyone was listening. No one was watching us, so I felt like I could speak freely.

"I'm a little scared. Actually, I'm really afraid. You've seen how girls like Karen act. She always cuts in front of me if we arrive at the cafeteria at the same time. It drives me crazy! I'm scared!"

I spoke in a low voice, like I was sharing a shameful secret. Suddenly, I felt someone behind me. I jumped and stepped back, startled.

"Easy, easy, it's just me."

I hadn't heard Emma arrive. She also spoke softly, in a very different tone from her usual "barking" (another weird word that really says something).

"We get it right, Lucie? It's normal to be scared. Fear sharpens your mind, triggers adrenaline, heightens your awareness. The players who say they're fearless? They're more dangerous to themselves. Remember that!"

She clearly hadn't understood what I was really talking about. Good. I was just as afraid of Karen as I was of my own reactions. Lucie played along.

"Yeah, you see my size? You think I'm not scared when a girl is twice my height and twenty kilos heavier?"

"There's no shame in accepting fear. I'm sure you already know that," Emma added. "The problem is when fear makes you freeze up. Two options: one, rely on your technique, the precise movements your body knows by heart, without thinking; two, face realistic but safe situations during practice. That's my job to organize. Sound good?"

Emma turned around and blew her whistle. Lucie gave me a pat on the shoulder, then took my hand and pulled me toward the field. Her hand was cool and a little rough. A warm flush swept through me—I felt reassured.

Touch rugby began. Then came the usual passing drills and technique routines. After that, we gathered for upper-body warm-ups. In a circle around one volunteer who led the exercises: neck, shoulders, torso, hips, arms—everything. Then, in pairs. I'd seen them do it, but actually doing it myself was something else. Hand games to slap each other; grabbing each other muscularly without knocking the other over; tackling position—same as for the scrum—alone against a partner's leg; then one-on-one scrummaging.

I was discovering it all, but I felt like a spectator in someone else's life. I was uncomfortable with all the physical contact—a reflex to pull away came with almost every move. Did my teammates notice? If they did, they didn't show it. At the same time, I told myself it was natural—to touch, to rub. My body remembered something like that from a long time ago. But the truth is, it was worse than that, and I could feel it rising again from deep inside. That's why I was so wary.

At that moment, I did everything I could to focus on the movements—on technique, like Emma had said. I was also lucky. I was paired with another girl my size, but more experienced. Her name was Alexandra. She had a real presence and enthusiasm. She often worked with the backs, though I didn't quite know what position she played. She also got along well with Lucie. All I knew was that she played behind the forwards, who were grouped into the pack—the ones who handled scrums and lineouts.

It was the first time I'd really spoken with her. She must have weighed the same as me, but with low shoulders and muscular thighs, she looked solid as a rock. She took the time to repeat each drill for me, the instructions and Emma's reminders, even if it meant fewer practices. Her tone was a bit sharp, but respectful. Her advice felt like orders, but I could tell she wanted to help.

When we moved on to four-person drills, we switched partners and practiced the ruck—a spontaneous scrum to fight for the ball, as Emma defined it. And bad luck for me, I didn't know any of the girls, except Karen. She walked up, and I saw that mean grin on her face. The instructions were clear: start from one corner of a square, leap over a tackle bag that represented a player with the ball, then face the opponent from the opposite corner. That opponent had to "clear out," meaning push you away so she could go over the bag and grab the ball. It was like a duel, and to me, it felt like a brawl.

Emma reminded us to keep low, flat back, head up. She repeated that it was about practicing tackling position, without going to ground. Despite my fear, despite Karen, I thought I was ready. I let the other pair go first to see how it was done. Then came my turn. I ran, took a big step over the bag, head starting to rise, still thinking about leg and back position, and then boom!

I was swept up! Karen had slammed into me with her full weight. It's hard to describe what I felt—and I'm not that light —but my breath was knocked out of me. I felt like I was flying —because I was—and then I hit the ground hard on my back. My head whipped back and cracked against the turf.

The pain was immediate. Above me, two of the other girls appeared, with flushed faces, but not Karen. Then Emma came over.

"Okay, ladies, give us space. Nothing to see here! I've got her. Fatimata, can you hear me? Don't move, okay?"

I was numb all over. My chest suddenly opened, and I gasped for a huge breath.

"Karen, to the sideline. We're going to talk. You two, join the others. Lucie, Alex, take over. You know what to work on and how."

She leaned towards me again.

"Don't try to move your head or sit up. Blink if you understand. I'm going to ask you some questions. Answer the best you can."

After a series of questions about what parts of my body I could move, she asked if I could sit up. I still felt dazed. A few minutes later, I got up on my own and slowly walked to the sideline. There, she asked another round of questions: any nausea? No? Headache? Then the date—day, month, year—my name. I quickly understood she was checking for a concussion.

Meanwhile, my hazy brain was overheating. Shame and anger flooded me. How could I have trusted so easily? I thought everyone would like me and be kind. I should've known better. This wasn't Karen's first time. I was mad at myself most of all. My blood boiled. I wanted to hit someone.

Emma had gone to the locker room to get ice. I didn't think for a second. I grabbed my stuff and ran. Not a jog—a sprint. I ran through the fading summer heat like I hadn't run in ages. Despite my blurred vision, the budding headache, the cramps in my stomach, I ran, trying not to think, but couldn't. The pain grew with every stride.

To calm down, I tried thinking of the warm house I lived in now. Maybe the magic would work. I focused on a few vivid details, hoping they'd help me forget the pain. Some had caught my eye the day I arrived at Santi and Marie's, after leaving the sanatorium: the frieze along the facade reminded me of something from my past, its ochre and pink patterns, and the little diamond-shaped openings in the wall. I could picture them perfectly as my feet pounded the pavement. I used to think those architectural details were just decorative—but I later learned the holes had been used to ventilate attics a long time ago.

That mental trick only lasted a few minutes. The cramps worsened. Cold sweats came. A mix of fear and rage pushed me to run faster still, even as the pain in my lower belly intensified. My breath and strides found a rhythm, and I didn't even watch where I was going. I let my body take over, but I sensed something was wrong. It wasn't just the heat or the head injury. I should have phoned Marie to ask her to examine me.

When I got home, I doubled over, puking onto the doormat, and felt something warm run down my thigh.

A moment later, I fainted.

CHINGUETTI, RAINY SEASON 2017

These past few weeks, they've been going to the doctor a lot. Almost every day. For Ada, her little sister. As a baby, it was chronic diarrhea. Now, it's dental infections and conjunctivitis. There's always something. She cries. She screams. She rolls on the ground. Because she'd rather be running around with the older kids. But in these cases, she has to follow quietly. Their father gave her a smack. She understood.

The health centre is nice. It's not red. It's egg-yolk yellow. Her grandmother says so. And it's clean. No sand or dust inside. It's cool in there. Feels like a vacation. Too bad running is forbidden. She and her friends would love to race through the hallways, play hide-and-seek. While her mother talks to the nurse, she pokes her head through the door. On the other side, the staff room. Actually, just a bare room with a worn-out couch and a table. But on that table, there's a television.

There's no TV at home. So it's like a miracle. She discovers France 24 or TV5 Monde. She steals fragments of life. With a bit of guilt. News reports, newscasts, variety shows— everything is worth watching. Every time, it's the same magic! As if the TV were always on. She can't take her eyes off the images. She loses track of time. Doesn't hear her mother calling. Doesn't see her come up behind her either. She's hypnotized. So much so that her mother has to smack her on the head to snap her out of it. She then lowers her head. She says nothing. She can't defend herself. She believes it's her reward for coming along. Simultaneously, guilt overwhelms her, for she has nothing. She wishes she had something. A sickness, but not too serious. Just so she could share that with Ada. She would feel less alone that way.

So, she has to take extra care of Ada. She's her big sister. She will protect her. On the way back from the clinic, she places herself at her sister's left side. She takes her hand, firmly, like it's her duty to. On the other side, her mother does the same. There, she'll never let go of her sister's hand again.

That same evening, the sun isn't so harsh. So they go out to the dunes. A bunch of children sitting and gazing at the dunes stretching into infinity. It's their horizon. What's beyond? More dunes? The television showed her other landscapes. To reach them, one would have to take the train of the National

Mining Company. Ride with the iron ore all the way to Nouadhibou? Or hop on the rickety bus that runs twice a day to Atar? It's like a dream. Many think about leaving. But that's not important at her age. Not yet.

They're more fascinated by water. Once a week. The ultimate joy: swimming in the nearby *gueltas*, which are becoming increasingly rare. They're like natural pools between rocks. The water is almost cold. To get there, you must be careful. The rocks along the path are sharp as razors. But it's also the path of scents. From the scorching sun to the soothing light. In pants or shirts, naked for the little ones. Everyone dives in. They splash about. They try to swim, heads above water. Sheer bliss. Wrinkled skin, they finally return home. Their bodies caressed by the evening breeze. By the scents perfuming their skin.

But they also have to watch out for AK-47 shells, which litter the ground. The older boys come sometimes. For the same reasons. But they come armed. They like to show off their firepower. It's a contest—who has the most powerful gun. They like shooting in all directions. It's their way of showing off. But Kalashnikovs aren't her thing. Their shooting always startles her. She prefers to head home as soon as they arrive. Most of the other children her age stay. Fascinated. No one sees the Kalashnikovs as dangerous. They're just part of the scenery.

Her grandmother disagrees. More than once, she warned her: never forget that they're made to kill. Game or human. For defence... or not. In the end, the result is the same.

TOULOUSE, SATURDAY, SEPTEMBER 30, 2023

This afternoon, I completed my little loop, as Santi calls it, in 45 minutes. Ten kilometres! While I was running, vivid memories came flooding in. They come in waves, more or less regularly. It's been like this since I ran away from the rugby practice two weeks ago. I'm confused—a barrier broke that day, maybe because of the blow to the head, or because my period came back after I don't know how many months. More and more, I feel like I left many things behind—deep things— as if roots I had refused to acknowledge were sprouting back to life. It's very strange and hard to explain, for me as well as for Marie and Santi.

The singer I'm listening to right now is proclaiming that she has no more roots. Is that possible? Is it even desirable?

I only got back to running this week, as per "the protocol," as they say, after my mild concussion. I have my route set out: I exit the house through the garden in the back, where I do some stretches to warm up. If there's no sign of a migraine, I jog to the front and start down the street, breathing deeply. I look at the bushes, sniff fragrant flowers, and sometimes catch the distant sound of a car. I jog those first few hundred metres, passing walkers, usually with their dogs.

Once I hit Camille Pujol Avenue, I begin to push my body with steady, regular strides, just to feel my muscles work. Then I turn at the intersection with Jean Chaubet Avenue, then left again onto Louis Plana Street, until I reach the ring road. Three streets further, on the right, there's a narrow lane that looks like a dirt path leading to a wasteland. I slip into this green passage that usually goes unnoticed. The trees form a kind of tunnel, their boughs crossing over.

If it has rained, then the earth and plants release their aromas more intensely, in waves. My stride lengthens, my eyes catch beams of sunlight piercing through the leaves, like flashes. The first few times, I tripped here and there on roots— a few scratches, but I just smile. As if there were no more roots, I keep a smooth, springy stride and focus on that. On my breathing too, especially the exhale. I turn inward.

From time to time, I hear rustling leaves. I jump and pick up the pace. Farther along, a cloud of butterflies rises in my wake —or birds. I almost leap into the puddles when there are any. I run in this timeless vortex, faster and faster, reaching that desired state. I move from one section of the green trail to another, in "crescendo" (what a beautiful Italian word, isn't it?), completely immersed in motion. I speed up, sensations intensify, and the ground, soft or firm, sends vibrations up my legs. I try to keep a light bounce and improve my strides each time, just a little more. There are sounds, yet it's silent inside.

The state I reach is indescribable. I feel like I'm in a cocoon, sealed and soundproofed. Total bliss. I forget everything—or rather, I let the film play in my head without trying to stop it or reflect. Santi and Marie helped me find the path to reach this state. It's part of the healing process. They're seasoned runners, but I've only stumbled into it by accident.

The silence breaks suddenly at the start of the final climb of my route because I'm almost home. My feet have remained on the ground during the run, but I feel as if I'd been lifted up and am now coming back down to earth. I check my stopwatch and wipe my face with my T-shirt, like always. But this time, Marie calls out from the side door porch:

"Nana, just in time! Phone call for you. A classmate from school!"

I barely had time to take my phone off airplane mode when I saw a message. Then I was holding another phone—our home phone. Someone really wanted to reach me.

"Hi, it's Aïcha. You didn't answer me!"

"Hi, sorry, I was out running."

Why did I feel the need to justify myself? Despite her approximate French, I could tell from her tone that she was annoyed.

"Can you confirm you're coming tonight, with the other girls. There'll be five of you. Half the basketball team."

"Yes, of course! Like I told you, my parents said yes. I'll be at your place at six. Do you want me to bring anything?"

"A pelo."

"A pillow? Okay, my pillow."

"And candy?"

"Yes, of course—the blue raspberry ones. The really sour ones."

"Thanks. Bye."

Just like that, she hung up. It felt strange correcting her French when I myself am always getting corrected—by teachers, by Santi, by Marie... They keep telling me: details matter. And I believe them. Could I really be getting that good?

I realized I had barely an hour to get ready. I'd take the tram a few streets over. Aïcha lives downtown, in an apartment complex with a pool and a gym. Her family came from East Africa a few months ago, through regular immigration channels —but with a lot of money—as "entrepreneurs." She's the only student I felt close to right away. Maybe her name influenced me... It's true, she reminded me of the other Aïcha—her mannerisms and her long hair.

In any case, she talks to everyone easily, unbothered about making mistakes in French. That's an asset, in my opinion, because it means we complement each other. She speaks faster than she thinks too, but she's kind and soft-spoken. While thinking about her, I finished showering and had to dry my hair. Ah, let the air do it, I told myself—my hair already covers my ears and it's braided anyway. I got dressed quickly and packed a small backpack with overnight stuff, a toiletry kit, and my pillow. Just had to stop and buy those candies—the ones we all liked, kind of like a trust token for this girls' night.

We were seven in the end, including me and half the basketball team. It felt a bit odd that we were all black girls. For several months, I'd gotten used to a more mixed environment, including at school. I quickly understood Aïcha was joining the team—she acted like one of them, laughed at their training stories and game recaps, even though she hadn't been there.

The ride was short.

To the music of Aaron Smith, we got into pajamas first— mandatory to look chill. Aïcha's parents weren't home, so we took over the living room. We sprawled on couches or the floor, gossiping about who was dating whom or confessing crushes. Then we shared our favourite influencers, and some brought out cigarettes, quickly followed by joints and hard liquor like tequila and vodka.

65

I didn't have much to say or do. I felt like a spectator. We stuffed ourselves with candy and chips—everyone had brought a bag. It was like no one had eaten all day! I didn't know my alcohol tolerance, even though I'd tried it before, always with adults. I took a glass like the others but only pretended to drink. I just wet my lips occasionally while the girls endlessly posed for photos and videos, which they immediately posted online.

Half-reclined on the couch, I wasn't hungry anymore, and it was only 7 p.m. Aïcha started dancing, then another joined in, and soon everyone was jumping around. She had two massive screens on the wall, side by side. It was impressive. She turned the sound up full blast as music videos played. After an hour of sweating and twisting, the doorbell rang. The pizza had arrived.

The girls went wild. Aïcha brought out more bottles. Joints were passed around. After that, my stomach was bursting and even though I hadn't drunk much, my head was spinning. Night fell, the world outside the residence grew quiet, and then Aïcha called out, "Everyone to the pool!"

Each girl found a corner to change. It was so loud—a real "cacophony" (I think of ducks when I hear this word)! We ran to the pool. So refreshing! The sun was setting and a strange pink light bathed the whole indoor pool. So magical! But the echo of the girls' shrieks began to tire me, so I lay down on a lounge chair.

Aïcha came over with a giant mixed-race girl. I knew she was the basketball team captain—just massive. Every part of her was disproportionately bigger than the rest of us, and Aïcha, already taller than me, only came up to her chest. They turned toward me. To avoid craning my neck, I stood up.

"You good? Having fun? This is Naziirah. You know her?"

"Yes."

The giant took over.

"Hey, we heard about your speed. I saw you in PE. Girl, you are *fast*. You're really athletic! And you're part of the community, you know? I think you'd fit right in on our team."

I was a bit surprised. I thought anyone could do any sport here.

"Thanks, but I already play rugby. I like it a lot…"

"Not with the school. And girl, what are you doing with *them*?"

"Well, I didn't really think about it. The team's pretty mixed. They like the same sport I do, so we play together. It made sense to join the team."

My tone had come out sharper than intended. But Naziirah carried on like nothing happened.

"Look at Aïcha. She's better off with us, right?"

Naziirah's huge head bobbed, as if to signal frustration. Aïcha nodded to confirm.

"So, your rugby friends—none of them are racist? They've accepted you without saying a word?"

I didn't know what to say. Should I bring up the incident during the first practice circle? The thing with Karen and her boyfriend in the cafeteria was already school gossip, but I never considered how others interpreted it. Were they just isolated incidents? Maybe. But not insignificant ones. Karen was just one player out of thirty or forty. And the coach had since put her in her place. No, I didn't think my teammates were racist.

"I like meeting people who are different from me, I guess."

"What?"

Aïcha had misheard—or pretended to.

"Even though I'd like to return to Mauritania one day, I came here to change my life. What about you, Naziirah? Where are you from?"

"Burkina Faso. Well, my parents immigrated. I was born here."

"Have you been to Africa?"

"Twice since I was born. Travel's expensive, especially for a family of six. We've got money, but still…"

"No need to apologize. I get it. Aïcha, you're Nigerian, right?"

"Yes, why?"

"When did you arrive?"

"Just before primary school. My parents thought it was the right time…"

"Well, okay then. I've found my community elsewhere. So thanks for the offer, but no."

This time, I answered sharply, on purpose. That was the last straw. They turned without a word. I didn't talk to them again for the rest of the night, except out of politeness before bed.

I couldn't fall asleep anyway. I was tired but uncomfortable. I wished I were somewhere else—gone and never seeing them again. I panicked for a moment. I left the room saying I needed the bathroom.

Sitting on the toilet, I thought. I felt wrong being here, so far from my bed. I wanted to leave, to escape, to block out their voices. Like that other time. I thought of my night terrors. I genuinely felt sick. Nauseous. A knot in my stomach. I made my excuses to Aïcha. This time, I wasn't alone, like in Atar. I called Santi and Marie.

A little worried, they came to pick me up right away. While waiting, sitting alone on the doorstep, I let my mind drift back to...

TOULOUSE, WEDNESDAY, OCTOBER 11, 2023

Some time ago, I discovered female rap. In the media, people often talk about male rappers, but rarely about female ones. That's a shame because it's powerful and it's good. I listen to a lot of different music, but right now, it's all about female rap, and it feels like it's opening up a whole new world for me. That's what I was thinking as I walked to the stadium, because I had finally ended up going back to rugby, but under certain conditions.

First, I had to see a doctor other than Marie, someone who had also played rugby in the past.

"Minor concussion confirmed and recovered from! Your daughter's got a hard head!"

Santi and Marie looked at each other, and I saw the love and pride in their eyes at that moment. It made me happy. And it was true, it wasn't my first blow to the head.

"So, can she return to rugby practice?"

"Yes, of course. I'll fill out a return-to-play note for the coach. You were wise to let her rest up for a few days. Making her take a break was a good precaution, though with minor concussions, we now recommend a fairly quick return to physical activity. It actually speeds up recovery, according to some very reliable studies. That said, it's what the protocol recommends anyway."

Nobody added anything, and I didn't mention that I had already resumed running. I didn't want to break the spell, but I knew they were the kind of people who had done a lot of research before making that decision. They wouldn't have taken the risk otherwise.

Second, in a fit of wounded dignity—or misplaced pride, according to Marie—I had decided that Lucie had to come talk to me first at school. She was in *Première* (grade eleven). Normally, the *Premières* didn't mix with the *Secondes* (grade ten students), but she did take the initiative. It happened right in front of everyone, at the cafeteria, during lunch.

I had already noticed that several players from the rugby team often ate together—maybe not every single lunch, but almost daily. Like me, each of them probably had clubs or meetings during the break, but they still made time to share that moment.

That day, Lucie caught me just as I was about to sit with the group from the integration class. Tanned, in jeans and a sweatshirt, her hair loose, she looked radiant. Surprised and flustered, I'm sure I blushed. I also stammered, uneasy about how I was looking at her, and afraid of how others might see me. Delighted by her invitation, I followed her when she asked me to join her and the other players. At the end of lunch, I promised I'd come to practice that evening. I mean, how could I say no?

Third, in the end, I really had to force myself to do it. In the excitement of sharing that meal with the rugby girls, I hadn't given it a second thought. But as the hours passed that afternoon, I began to hesitate. By the time I got home from school, I had changed my mind. I didn't want to go back. A part of me, one I didn't fully understand, was resisting. Another pride thing.

Sitting at the kitchen table for a snack, Marie and I talked, and she reassured me.

"Sweetheart, I also took some hits. Getting knocked around is part of rugby. And I always got back up. What matters more is how you respond to it."

"Yeah, I get it. I'm not ashamed of the hit. I'm ashamed that I ran away, that she intimidated me."

"Ashamed that you ran instead of standing your ground. OK, it's true that's not what rugby is about. That's not the lesson we want you to learn. You're here to learn, right? So take it as a lesson! Come back smarter, stronger. That's where your pride should be!"

As the Rolling Stones blared in the background, Marie continued. She knew what she was talking about. She started playing rugby when she was sixteen, after ten years of ballet and a bit of volleyball. She had loved it, and only stopped because of her job and all the travel it required. Her words weren't harsh. I understood, and during the drive, I realized I was glad we'd had that conversation.

When I arrived at the field, Emma, the coach, pulled me aside.

"I didn't appreciate your behaviour the other day. Running off like that. Honestly! It's also a matter of respect. Toward me, since I invest my time in you. Toward your teammates, who count on you."

"But I don't even know if I'll make the team!" I replied, a bit defensively.

"That's not the point. A team has A-squad, B-squad. Big, small, tall, short, slow, fast, glasses, no glasses, everyone has a place in the group. On the field, your teammates are going to sweat blood for you. And you'll do the same for them. They'll go into the thick of it, draw off defenders, take risks so you can carry the ball farther. Risk a tackle. Risk a cheap shot. And they'll get back up, believe me. For you, for me, for the team, for the beauty of the game."

Generosity and beauty—two concepts people don't usually associate with rugby. But those words convinced me. I felt that I was part of the team, no matter what.

Karen apologized in front of all the girls at the beginning of practice, during the team huddle. It was clearly a bit forced, but I accepted her apology in good faith and we gave each other a hug. After that, I threw myself into practice like a starving maniac. I was even a little impressed with myself—despite two weeks without practice, thanks to my daily runs, I had actually gained endurance!

Practice sessions followed one after the other, and I quickly got back into the rhythm. New sensations appeared—not in my legs (though I know I still need to strengthen my ankles and knees to improve pivoting). Side-steps or dummy passes can't be improvised. No, it was in my hands. Now I could feel where my hand was on the ball without even looking. I could feel the ball spinning off my fingertips when I snapped it; my hips were now part of that movement, giving it more power. I still need to build upper-body strength to make longer passes, but things are feeling good.

The cherry on the cake (such a French expression!)—five minutes of kicking practice in front of the goalposts at the beginning and end of every session convinced everyone that I had the makings of a kicker. Alex even shouted every time, "You're on fire today!"

During the end-of-practice games, we now play "tag rugby." I pushed myself because I wanted to conquer my fear of contact. It was torture resisting the urge to pull back, not trying to avoid the opponent's charge. Practice after practice, I faced it, accepted being touched, hit, taken down. I was succeeding, but in doing so, I sometimes lost my focus when receiving passes. Arm outstretched, fingers aimed at my teammate, I would watch the player facing me too closely and then miss moving my hands to catch the ball.

Knock-on—and ball to the other team. That's how Karen's prophecy came true!

"Knock-on! No scrum, red team, advantage blue. Play!" called out Emma, who was refereeing.

I was clutching my hand. The pain was sharp and localized.

"Hey, I twisted my finger!"

It was my right ring finger (I remembered the name because it's where you wear a wedding ring). But no one was listening. Across from me, Alex immediately kicked the ball low. She continued her run, recovered the ball, and scored the try. And there I was, still holding my hand, feeling a bit ridiculous.

"Nice play, blue team! Great instinct! Fatimata, are you okay? Go strap your fingers and come back quickly for the last few minutes of practice."

Lucie ran over to me. She walked me to the sideline, near the water spigot. She took the first aid kit—which looked empty—and pulled out a roll of tape like a magician pulling a rabbit out of a hat.

"Show me your hand. Which finger? Ah! Yeah, I see. Whoa —it's already swollen. Run it under cold water."

Then I reached out my left hand. Gently, she took it and dried the moisture with her training shirt. I felt her fingers on my skin. They were a bit rough, but it was pleasant. She wrapped the tape delicately. I was watching her, and she looked back at me—openly, clearly. A wave of warmth washed over me, like a window had opened onto an unknown land, a welcoming place reaching out to me. I felt a strange flutter, down in my belly.

"Ice it for fifteen minutes when you get home. If you have an arnica-based pain-relief cream, apply that too. Immobilize the finger, like I just did, for the next two practices. But keep doing the ball-handling drills, I showed you, at home and walking to practice."

I kept looking at her, saying nothing. I was entranced. I felt like I was floating and had only half-listened to her instructions. My lack of response must've made her think I was skeptical—but not in the philosophical sense—because she insisted in a caring tone. She wanted to reassure me. It was sweet, but for me, it went far beyond that.

"Your fingers will regain strength and mobility faster than if you keep them inactive and bandaged all the time. It's strengthening. Physiotherapy tricks. We've all had this kind of injury at some point. Don't worry about it."

She had finished the taping, but her hand still held mine, and I wasn't worried at all. I was just elsewhere, my thoughts swirling, unable to settle. My dark thoughts, my traumatic memories vanished during that moment between us.

The final whistle of practice blew, startling me. The session had ended, and we hadn't returned to the field.

"You'll be more careful next time?"

The question sounded more like a warning, like something you'd say to a child. I felt a bit ashamed, especially knowing I'd be subjected once again to Lucie's double check-up *and* the family doctor. Otherwise, no rugby! No, not now, I told myself on the walk home. I'm not giving up again over this. I've worked too hard, Nothing will stop me.

And despite myself, these thoughts brought me back to the path of exile from Mauritania, carrying its load of memories. Like Rousseau, I realized that walking was fertile ground for reveries, and nightmares.

NOUADHIBOU, MAURITANIA, OCTOBER 2022

If her memory sometimes plays tricks on her, her body does not. It remembers all too well. Instantly. Through the skin, the nose, the ears. It's strange. The paved sidewalks. A rough, cold concrete, so different from the sand or the dirt. Potholes. She's panting. Her feet hurt. She's still running in her mind as she sits down on the ground facing the ocean. She's exhausted. Mentally too. She's been running for a week to save her life.

She left Atar and Mohamed Ould Obeid, her husband, as if pursued by a demon. In the middle of the night, a few days after her wedding night. After making sure he had paid her parents their due. And they had paid theirs. All in secret, from the other wives, from the children, from the slaves. She left as she had come. With nothing. Or almost nothing. In a large handkerchief, she carries her jewellery. Every little piece given by that man three times her age. Every tiny earring, every finely wrought necklace or bracelet. Each one of those objects, with which he bought her body.

The smells of Nouadhibou invade her nostrils. Salt, tide, dried seaweed, and fish. The big-leaved palm trees too, when you move a bit away from the port. And the aroma of roasted coffee. A hint of music from a café corner. The foghorns of the big ships in the bay. The shouting of the fishermen tying up their boats after a day at sea. Scents and sounds transformed by the evening's coolness. It's almost a kind of pleasant music.

Nouadhibou, the northwestern port. A dream for many. And the gateway to Spain, to Europe, to the rest of the world. She doesn't know much about all of that. A daughter of the desert, she has never seen so much water, except on television. It's frightening. All this water, moving endlessly. She wonders if this is where it all begins? But where to begin? She knows no one. She just wants to get far away.

At the port, she's in the right place, in the early morning breeze that brings with it the smell of fish. It makes her hungry. She's been saving on food these past few days. She's already lost weight. A meal will come later. Maybe. She has other things to do.

She approaches the quay. Here, it stinks—a damp stench, a mix of curdled milk and gasoline... A young black man is sitting on the quay, legs dangling. He's wrapping something around a makeshift hook. Maybe a bug. It disgusts her a bit.

79

She gets closer: a viscous paste leaks from the creature as it's pierced. The boy looks to be about her age. He has a little portable radio next to him. He sings along with a funny accent. She catches a few phrases in French: *"Ti achètes misique," "ti a maison au village"*... But sometimes the words are incomprehensible: *"garba man," "y a fobi," "taises."*

He turns around. Says hello. He speaks a French different from hers. The same accent as the singer. It's like a symphony of rolling pebbles. But she mostly understands him. His name is Abou. He's Senegalese. Yes, like Ismaël Lô. "De Saint-Louis," he adds. She can't believe her ears.

"Abou de Saint-Louis, is that your name?" He replies, "No, silly, that's where I was born. That's where I lived. Saint-Louis is the old colonial capital!" He leans closer, whispering mysteriously: "I come from a sunken city... but I'll tell you about that another day! My name is Abou Ba. And yours?"

He smiles with all his teeth. Soon she learns he's leaving too. He knows the way. A pirogue. Wider and longer than the fishermen's boats. Destination: the Canary Islands, a thousand kilometres away. A gateway to Europe. They talk a lot. Each in their own broken dialect. Over the months, he'll teach her his Senegalese French and she'll teach him hers. Strange and new expressions: *"entre-coucher," "faire des poses," "faut fléblé"*...

He also teaches her that the government has tightened things up. In recent years, they made a deal with the Spanish to stop migrants. New laws, more police—all against people like him. And her. Poor people who just dream of something better. Or elsewhere. Which is the same thing.

Nothing will stop Abou and his companions from leaving Africa. Better to die trying over there than wait for death here, he tells her. That evening, they share grilled sea bream over a beach fire. He speaks in grandiose sentences:

"You are like joy. You are like a smile. You are the sign I was waiting for."

But he also tells her about a friend's cousin who settled here after more than two years of wandering between Côte d'Ivoire, Mauritania, Senegal, and Cameroon. After the authorities finally offered him a job. Now he's a teacher. He has his woman, his own place. And he doesn't want to leave.

She asks Abou why he wants to leave. He doesn't answer. Even though she's the only (young) woman among fifty men, she will board that pirogue.

Now it's total darkness. A moonless night—the best kind, the smuggler confirmed. He put them in the pirogue, and pointed in a direction with his finger, somewhere off to the left. "That way!" he said and vanished. Swallowed by the night, with half her jewellery.

She feels awful. A constant nausea since they boarded. Hours go by. There's nothing left in her stomach—she's vomited it all. But still, the nausea. She's been told it's seasickness. She no longer asks how far they've come. She quickly understands no one knows. It becomes day. Then night again. Then day once more.

Each of them rows until they collapse. The blisters on her fingers have burst. Her throat is dry and her tongue swollen. She sees black spots. Suddenly, one of them moves. It's getting closer. The other passengers are shouting. With the last of her strength, she joins in. Maybe her strange voice will be heard this time.

"We're here! Help! Help us!"

Abou collapses into her arms.

"We made it, Nana, we..." His sentence is cut off by the loudspeaker from the approaching coast guard vessel. The message is in Arabic.

They're being taken back to where they started. Their escape attempt ends here.

TOULOUSE, SATURDAY, OCTOBER 21, 2023

As soon as I got back from practice, Marie confirmed that my finger was broken. And Santi, nodding sagely, also cast a mock-expert glance at it. So Lucie had been right, beautiful Lucie, and sure enough, the bruise changed colour over the days. It would fade eventually. It wasn't my first. The problem was that I had piano practice and wanted to stick to it, at least fifteen minutes a day!

Now, thanks to Franck (a lot) and my daily practice (a little), I had started to play a few pieces with both hands. I didn't want to give that up, but I had to go back to practicing with one hand, because unfortunately, it was my right hand— and I'm right-handed! I took it as a chance to improve my left hand and develop my "ambidexterity" (thank you, Santi, for the vocabulary!).

And rugby? I got upset. I defended my case by confronting Marie (I pictured myself literally grabbing her):

"A broken finger will never stop me from practicing!"

"Have you even tried to play? It's your right hand, after all."

"Yes, I can still spin the ball. Almost normally."

Marie looked skeptical, which annoyed me.

"If it's not treated properly, you risk injuring it again. And you'll get arthritis when you're old."

"In how many years? When does someone start getting old? I'm still young."

"If you ask me, we start aging the day we're born, so…"

That was Santi's kind of humour, always chiming in! Marie knew him too well to laugh, but I laughed willingly. He managed to calm me down with his six-foot-two frame and curly hair that always made him look like a mad scientist. He likes giving little philosophy lessons, even if it sometimes makes him seem a bit full of himself, but he's never condescending.

He went over to the Bose speaker, the small Bluetooth amp.

"Here, let's listen to some local music for a change, shall we?"

I really liked philosophy—he knew that. For the last two weeks, he'd started placing a book on my nightstand every day, by authors with funny names (Epictetus, Epicurus, Seneca, Lucretius…). The sceptics, the stoics, and the "whole gang" (sounds cool, doesn't it?). We had already started talking about them, and when he spoke to me, I felt smarter.

"But you, you don't look like you're aging! You look young."

"I'm a fake young person, believe me. It's like my weight. No matter how much I eat, I stay skinny."

"That's true, I've never seen you gain a pound, I replied, laughing."

"I'm a fake skinny person, you see?"

"You mean you're actually fat?"

"Well, not exactly... But if you weigh me, you'll see I'm around ninety kilos."

"Huh?"

"Well, look at my shape. What does that tell you?"

"That you have a lot of muscle? Since muscle weighs more than fat."

"Or that my bone density is higher than average. I must have steel-reinforced bones!"

Once again, he had me laughing. The fact is, he was muscular, he stayed in shape by running whenever he could, and he practiced other sports too. Wherever he travelled, he'd go for a run, that's what he'd told me. He also played music—guitar. He dabbled in everything! I'd quickly come to like his personality, and every day more so.

"In any case, you two remind me of my teachers, Marc and Jessica."

"Why's that?"

And then I launched into a long story, something I never would have thought myself capable of a few months earlier. Marc and Jessica also worked really well together, they complemented each other, each with their own subjects, but in harmony. Thanks to them, I had caught up a lot, and I felt like I was making quick progress. They'd told me that next year I could probably join the regular curriculum if I kept progressing like this.

I'd discovered the arts, both theory and practice, which complemented my lessons with Franck—drawing, painting, sculpture. I really enjoyed it, and I was even a little less afraid of doing my theatre class, scheduled for next term. Still, performing in front of an audience gave me the jitters. In physical education, I was less self-conscious; my strengths were beginning to show, as Jessica had noted. For example, I could dribble and score goals when we played soccer, even though in the locker room I still avoided changing in front of others. I just couldn't, unlike some girls whom I found shameless.

But there was actually a big difference between my adoptive parents and my teachers. At the end of our last class, Jessica and I had a real conversation. I learned—or rather, understood—that Marc and Jessica weren't a couple, not like Santi and Marie, anyway. What a surprise! And that wasn't all...

"We work together, but as partners, you understand? We get along very well. I like him a lot as a colleague and friend. But, Nana, I prefer women."

I wasn't sure I understood. I liked girls too. And I liked boys as well. Based on the few memories I had from my life in Mauritania, I'd had male friends all my childhood. The memory of Abou resurfaced, painful and joyful, with the last images of our shipwreck. I closed my eyes for a second to compose myself, then continued:

"Why are you telling me this?"

"You look uncomfortable."

"Yes, I think some girls go too far. They walk around completely naked in front of everyone."

"And you find that shocking, I understand. You'll get used to it. People here are less self-conscious about those things. Mostly, we pay less attention to them. No one will ever force you to undress in public, okay? But that's not what I meant. What I want to say is that it's okay to be attracted to a girl one day and to a boy the next. You absolutely have the right to fall in love with a girl."

"I'm not looking for sex!"

"I'm not saying you are. I don't know anything about that, and I don't want to know, because that's your private life. I'm talking about emotions, feelings, friendship, and love."

"Where I am from, it's forbidden to love someone of the same sex."

"Yes, but here, it's allowed."

"You're not making any sense! And besides, it's disgusting!"

I turned my back and ran away. Thankfully, it was the last class of the day. As soon as I got home, I changed. I didn't want to know, didn't want to think about it—but deep down, I admit I knew…

The wooded path was waiting for me, with its soothing shade and intoxicating scents, so I went out to run my rage away. I dove into the green cocoon that insulated me from the world and my worries. As usual, I started with light, bouncing strides—I was angry. A bit later, I realized something had shifted deep inside me. A shiver ran through me at the thought, a shiver that reminded me of others, the moments of intimacy I had always pushed away. With Aïcha, in Atar. More recently, with Lucie. Yes, Lucie. Lucie, Lucie, Lucie… Every time she came close, my body—and my heart—reacted. All of this was spinning in my mind as I ran.

When Lucie was near, I felt warmer, my heart beat a little faster. Just the thought of seeing her again, just thinking of her now, made me feel something in my stomach. All of a sudden, I had a premonition. A shadow slipped behind me, or rather, a malevolent spectre trying to grab me. It smelled of rancid onion and male sweat. I felt a trail of cold sweat run down my spine. My mind was spiralling, so instinctively I ran faster.

I hadn't yet reached the halfway point, but I picked up my pace. I leaned forward slightly, shifted my weight onto the balls of my feet, and pushed my body ahead. I pumped my arms, as if pulling on a rope, and sprinted down the tunnel, running as fast as I could to leave everything behind me.

TOULOUSE, WEDNESDAY, NOVEMBER 15, 2023

In the past few weeks, the coach clearly split the team in two—at least during the central part of practice. On one side, the pack, the forwards; on the other, the backs... and me in the middle. At least, that's how I felt, not really belonging to either group.

Emma first placed me with Alex, the fly-half, and a dozen other players. At first, I was glad not to have to train with Karen. I thought everything would go fine. Then I got sent to the forwards... with Lucie, which was some consolation. The explanation I was given didn't really convince me, but who was I to claim I knew better than the coach? Marie was quick to remind me of that, even after I repeated the conversation I had with Emma.

"Listen, Fatimata, nothing serious, but you're dropping too many balls during practice games. Too many knock-ons—it's becoming a concern."

"Yeah, I know, but everyone's yelling around me, it scrambles my brain, and I panic. I'm really sensitive to noise, but it'll pass—it's just a matter of time. And my finger healed... though not completely!"

"That's true, I get it. Still, let me remind you: at inside centre or wing, on top of defending, you have to pass and receive the ball a lot, and run with it. That's your role."

"I've improved my tackling, and my passes are okay, aren't they?

"They're not bad. Listen, I don't want this to feel like a punishment. But until things get better and your finger fully heals, you'll train with the forwards. You'll handle the ball less, which might help. I've been watching your kicks. You're shaping up to be one of our go-to kickers, if you're up for it. You still need more practice, though. I want you to train kicking from increasingly oblique angles, still from the 22-metre line, but moving farther from the posts each time. Got it? And also start practicing drop goals. Alex will help you. Keep doing your sessions at the beginning and end of practice, but add five more minutes. As for the rest, we'll see in time. Anyway, a little versatility is good.

No way! How could she believe training with the "heavies" would make me a better back? I suddenly wanted to tell her to shove it. "Get lost!" (I love that expression, even if I don't really see where the insult is.) But the urge quickly passed. Arguing with my coach and running away again was not an option.

So, I dragged myself over to them, slipping into the group like an intruder. My build was unlike any of the other forwards, who were either shorter or taller. And I weighed twenty kilos less than the lightest of them! The ones I resembled most were the flankers—tireless runners and tacklers, Lucie said, trying to comfort me. Unfortunately, my tackling technique was still beginner level. No way I'd be able to play that position anytime soon. They were experienced girls, as Emma had explained, and I could see why. Once again, my only real consolation was Lucie, who spent most of her time training with us as scrum-half.

And, the cherry on top, I had to train with Karen "the cube," since she played front row. She was the hooker, a key position, especially in scrums and lineouts. After the assault, she had been benched for two weeks. At school, when she saw me, she'd change direction, or if she couldn't avoid me, she'd turn her back. On the rugby field, luckily, we hadn't faced each other since. Emma and Lucie had made sure of that. And now, I was supposed to scrum with her? It felt like *I* was the one being punished. She too could go to hell.

"The cube" gave me a dark look as I joined the forwards. I was sure she wanted to work with me as little as I did with her, but we had no choice.

So, I trained for scrums first as a prop, right next to her! Her armpit was at face level! I had to make the right moves at the right time, in sync with everyone else. Bend, touch, play! It looked easier from the outside. Each play, I got completely crushed—a total disaster! On both sides, the scrum collapsed because of me. As the drills went on, the grunts turned into complaints and protests; my teammates were starting to get really fed up.

So I tried second row. In lineouts, my explosiveness and light weight actually helped, and the girls encouraged me. But again, once we returned to scrums, I lacked the power. Another failure. My neck and shoulders were burning. I was on the verge of breaking. I'd had more than enough.

Eventually, Emma tried me as a flanker, and things seemed to go better at first. My right shoulder was strong enough to hold the pressure just long enough to keep the scrum up for the few seconds needed for Lucie to get the ball out. At least one person was happy with me, and not just anyone! That was enough for me. Lucie mattered more than all the others combined.

The problem was what came next. As soon as the ball came out, I understood that I had to quickly detach either to join the attack (if we had possession) or to set up in defence—ready to sprint and tackle any opponent who tried to break through. In both cases, I was quick off the mark, but at contact, I crumbled. Between the missed tackles and my (temporary) inability to clean out properly at the rucks, I admit it was pitiful.

Still, I felt I'd learned a lot. But my execution lacked strength and efficiency.

After a week of effort, Emma asked me to speak with her after practice.

"How are you, honey?"

"Uh... I wouldn't say great. I don't belong with the forwards, Emma."

"I think we've come to the same conclusion. Listen, I have a solution for you."

I expected her to send me back to the backs. I forgot one detail: I was about to be disappointed.

"You know games start next week, right?"

"Oh, yeah?"

I actually did know. The girls talked about nothing else.

"At the club, we never deny anyone the pleasure of playing rugby. But from now on, practice won't be with forty players anymore. We also play rugby sevens here. You've seen it before, right? The national team is one of the best in the world."

"Yeah, I know. It's Olympic rugby."

"There's no championship, but there are two to four tournaments a year. It's a different vibe. I'd like you to take part."

"That's the B team, right?"

"No, it's the sevens team. Not a B or lower team. There'll be about fifteen of you, who've trained with the others from the start, who have other strengths, like running fast, but who'll develop in a different way, in a different setting."

"Because we're the worst?"

"Let's say, the newest, for the most part. Not necessarily the worst. There are some older girls, too. Like you said, it's just a matter of time before you improve enough. The door is never closed. Practices will be on the same days, just after the fifteens."

"Hmm."

"You'll love it, I promise. You've got something the others don't, Fatimata. A *je-ne-sais-quoi*… You're not aware of it, but you really could bring something special to the sevens team."

I didn't believe a word of it, but I couldn't find anything to say—not even anger. I just managed to mutter a flat "thanks," holding back tears. I felt like an old sock thrown in the trash. I'd only see Lucie between sessions or at school now! And Alex? Who would look after me now?

For a few hours, the desire to play rugby left me completely. The walk home was one of the saddest of my life. The sun was setting as I left Les Argoulets, and my thoughts drifted toward skies just as bleak. I sank into the oncoming darkness, heavy with buried memories, and regrets.

Christmas is fast approaching! For the past few weeks, ghosts of the past have occupied a part of my thoughts, and I feel literally haunted. I had to resign myself to talking to the psychologist—that helped me keep going with schoolwork, seeing my friends at school or at rugby. I had even nearly forgotten Christmas, *the* family holiday! Unforgivable.

So I'm feeling torn, just as the season of parties is beginning. It's not that I don't care, but it's like there's a pressure to celebrate *before*. Before what, exactly? It's as if everyone's scrambling to have fun together because they'll soon leave to be with their families. And my family? Where are they? Who are they?

In Mauritania, we didn't really celebrate Christmas: no tree, no Santa, no midnight mass, no presents… None of it fit the life there. Did I regret that? I thought I'd moved on, but now it's coming back, and I think about it more and more. Do they think I'm dead? What's become of my little sister? And my grandparents? Will I ever see them again before they die?

In the end, I decided to share some of these questions with my new family over dinner. Marie and Santi listened attentively; I saw emotion in their eyes, even tears. Bobette whimpered and snuggled up next to me. They already knew part of my story, the part I'd chosen to share, but it had stayed between us until now. They offered to look into it, since they knew a lot of people working around the world, including in West Africa. Santi boasted about it often enough.

"Do you remember your parents' address?" Marie asked.

"You mean the town? Yes, Chinguetti. I don't think I can be more specific. There are no street names, or at least, I don't think there are."

"No problem, I understand. We can still fish around for some info, if you're okay with that."

"Unless you'd rather do it yourself, Santi added. We understand. Really! We were just waiting for you to bring it up first. We don't want to force your hand."

"Or have you leave us. You know we think of you as our daughter, but that doesn't mean you have to feel the same."

"Feel the same?"

"Yes, the reverse, if you like. If you don't think of us as your parents, that's okay. After all, your real parents are still alive. They surely miss you."

Santi's bummed-out look hit me. I'd really put my foot in it (not on purpose, though!). I didn't want them to think I saw them as strangers. Even though there were still so many missing pieces in the puzzle, deep down, I was convinced I'd chosen to leave on my own. No one had pushed me. I must have understood what that meant at the time, but living it was another story.

"I'm the one who wanted to change my life, to start over. I was ready to die for it. In fact, I almost did, didn't I? Abou really did die for it. And all the others. You found me and saved me, and I *do* think of you as my parents. I just have some questions."

"Are you ready to contact your family?" Santi asked.

"No."

"Okay. What do you want to do?"

"Nothing."

The conversation ended on that note, and honestly, I almost wished I could forget the whole thing, even though I could clearly see that Santi and Marie had "bittersweet" expressions (I'm using that word because I like it, though I'm not sure it's the right one). My cheeks were burning, but I forced myself not to storm off, or ignore their advice, or block out the thoughts I'd just voiced. We finished dinner in silence, heavier than usual, each lost in our own thoughts.

Another annoying thing about Christmas here is the frenzy over gifts and kindness. It's like you *have* to give presents to everyone and act happy and upbeat. Forced joy! Sometimes, it all feels fake, and I get dizzy from the hypocrisy. Other times, when I'm with classmates, I give in and get just as excited as the rest. Shopping, spending—it's part of fitting in for a migrant girl, isn't it?

So, I made a list and scheduled outings to buy gifts. Between homework, school clubs (I finally joined the Model UN!), rugby practices, daily running, and piano, my days were full, and I wasn't complaining.

On top of all that, several parties were planned in the lead-up to the holidays. I had to choose, since they were *only* on Fridays or Saturdays! My first pick was my class's party, which included a dinner organized by the teachers and then an unofficial after-party. Aïcha had sent out the invitation two weeks earlier. It would be held once again at her place, in her building with the pool. There was also the rugby dinner, organized by the club, followed by a private "after-party" at one of our teammates' houses. Alexandra had invited everyone. And both the sevens and fifteens teams had their own parties.

And then the Model UN club was heading to one of its two conventions of the year during the same period: a three-day trip with workshops, committee work, plenary sessions—and two nights away. Fifteen teens aged sixteen to eighteen, two hundred kilometres from home, no parental supervision. I couldn't even imagine what that would be like! I had never had such a full schedule before Christmas. I marked off every weekend in my planner. I was excited and terrified because it was all so new.

And tonight was one of those nights! I was late getting ready for the last party before the holidays. Nervous and trembling, it seemed like I was dropping everything I was holding on to. For a rugby player, that's the ultimate irony. Still, I'd gained confidence in my passes, my runs, even my kicks while playing sevens. The field was bigger, so there was less contact. That meant more chances to use my speed. And I had become "versatile" (Emma's word). When someone was tackled and went down, the ball had to come out quickly, so any of us could then play scrum-half. Our first tournament of the season was set for the start of the break, and everyone on the team was hyped after all those months of training. December flew by, just as wildly as I'd expected.

I admit, I was happy to be part of all these social events. It meant I belonged, at least a little. I felt lucky, almost too lucky. Did I really deserve it? The more the parties and weeks went by, the worse I felt. I had enough experience now—dancing (a lot), drinking (a bit), weed (barely)—and I enjoyed it less and less. Why? I didn't know. I kept thinking about it while pulling on a tight cotton dress that reached just below my knees. It showed off more of my curves than I liked, and I didn't want to draw attention to my chest, which I already thought too big—so no padded bra. It was my second time wearing the dress. The first had been at Aïcha's place. Initially, I'd worn that kind of outfit as a challenge, on Marie's suggestion—to break away from sweatpants and jeans. Alex and Lucie had said the same. But tonight, I just wanted to.

I ran to the bathroom mirror to grab "Rouge Allure" by Chanel. I applied the dark, discreet lipstick I'd chosen myself. I was so proud. I did the edges with a lip liner, filled in the centre, and cleaned up the smudges with a Q-tip soaked in makeup remover. Marie had taught me that trick. She'd also shown me how to apply mascara and shape my eyebrows. I adjusted my hoop earrings. My dreads ended in small coloured beads. On the outside, I looked pretty good. Inside, I wasn't sure who that girl in the mirror really was.

Time stood still (a beautiful phrase I learned in English). I was about to lose myself in thought when my phone buzzed and lit up. A text. Lucie was outside my house! She'd just gotten her learner's permit and was driving her parents' car. She'd offered to pick me up for the last party before the break and the sevens tournament. I'd accepted without even thinking.

Alex was hosting, and both teams would be there. As for Lucie, I'd seen her at school a few times, but always around other people—at lunch or in the hallways. We crossed paths on the field. Her practice ended when mine began. We chatted each time, but only small talk. I felt like the words we spoke didn't reflect what we really wanted to say. But this time, we'd be alone, just the two of us, in her car.

My heart leaped as I walked out the door. My hands got clammy, and I suddenly felt the urge to stare at my feet.

"Hi Nana. You look amazing in that dress! I've never seen you wear it."

"Uh, yeah, thanks. It's only the second time I've put it on."

"You should wear dresses more often to school. Let me see your face."

She flicked on the dome light as I sat in the passenger seat. Without warning, she leaned over, placed her hand under my chin, and gently tilted my head up. The touch sent a jolt through me. I flinched instinctively. She kept looking at me, unfazed.

"Don't be scared! What lipstick is that? It's gorgeous! It suits you really well. It highlights your lips, without overdoing it."

"Okay, thanks. It's Chanel. I'll show you it later. Shall we go?"

I was flustered, panicking. I hadn't even given her a single compliment, and she was so beautiful. She wore slim, light-coloured pants and a lime-green turtleneck. Her tan from summer still lingered, highlighting her freckles. Her thick, shoulder-length hair was held back by a simple green headband, and it smelled amazing! She wore hoop earrings too! Her makeup was even more subtle than mine, except for her lips. She wore a bold orange-red lipstick that I couldn't stop staring at.

"Do you like English pop from the 80s?"

103

"Uh, what? Yeah, I listen to everything."

"Okay, check this out, and tell me if you like it. It'll get us in the mood."

You make me feel that way. I wasn't used to that kind of music, but it was catchy, I had to admit. We "peeled off" (another Santi expression); her driving was sporty, but she seemed totally at ease. I focused all my energy on staying upright through the turns, my right hand clenching the door handle. It gave me a good excuse not to turn toward her, even though I sometimes tipped in her direction and couldn't help touching her.

After taking the ring road, we were out of the city in minutes. Just before entering Alex's parents' property, Lucie had told me the view was stunning from the terrace—it overlooked the Garonne Valley. We parked next to a dozen other cars lining the path. As soon as I stepped out, the thump of bass music hit me, so loud! No matter how many parties I went to, I never got used to it. I was still haunted by years of being screamed at. Right then, I felt like an impostor crashing a party not meant for me.

Multi-coloured string lights in the trees lit the way. We followed them to the entrance. Several people stood outside, talking, drinking, smoking. We knew most of them, and the rest were boyfriends or girlfriends, so the greetings were friendly. The front door stood open, inviting us in. The music got louder—not unbearable, but definitely coming from the back. It was dark, but I quickly made out bottles and glasses covering every surface. I crossed a large room where people were dancing. We greeted a few players we recognized in the shadows. Lucie was just ahead, leading the way, sometimes taking my hand to keep me close.

We stepped out into the backyard—a vast lawn full of dancers. At the far end, a small stage with a DJ. Huge speakers throbbed with a hypnotic beat. In the middle of the crowd, I spotted Alex, totally wild. She was always like that, but even more so tonight. The moment she saw us, she ran over and threw her arms around us. Clearly, she'd been drinking, and it made her even more affectionate and talkative.

"Lucie, Nana, finally! The party's on fire. Great, you came. Grab a drink! I have so much to tell you about what's happened tonight."

She pulled us to the side, where tables were set up with every kind of alcohol, juice, and soda. Within seconds, I had a drink in my hand and was clinking glasses. But as usual, I didn't really plan to drink. I was always afraid of what could happen. Back in Mauritania, of course, it was totally forbidden. Now, I just wanted to stay in control. Unlike Lucie and Alex, who downed several drinks in a row.

Then the three of us headed to the dance floor!

I danced for hours. I forgot my impostor syndrome. I thought of nothing but Lucie. Lucie dancing in front of me. Lucie moving in sync with me, and me with her. We swung our arms and hips together. I couldn't take my eyes off her. She was all I saw. Just the music and her, drawing closer and closer. I did nothing to stop it. A euphoric rush I'd never known surged through my body. I was drunk without drinking, drunk on the freedom to choose who I wanted. Lucie's emerald eyes locked me in, I was helpless. It was late when we kissed, for the first time.

I'm still on cloud nine after what happened the night before last, though I really should have seen it coming. Or maybe I'd pretended not to notice it, not to acknowledge my attraction to Lucie? Part of me is relieved that the uncertainty is gone, even though another part of me still resists—probably the part raised in Islam back in Mauritania. That part still believes this is madness, that it's not possible, that I'm straying.

Anyway, I spent all day Saturday doing nothing, just watching silly videos online, but I could feel my energy bubbling underneath. No one at home asked me any questions, I didn't talk about it with anyone, and Lucie hasn't contacted me.

Today is the first tournament of the season, and we're hosting it. That's the upside of playing for a top-tier club. It has more resources, like multiple fields, to organize this kind of event, which welcomes around ten teams from all over the region, confirming its status as a major club.

The holidays are in two weeks. Marie, Santi, and I still need to finish our Christmas shopping, like everyone else. "Not this weekend," Marie declared at lunch with a half-resigned, half-amused tone. "We'll do it last minute, like always." The three of us are way too excited to think about anything else, and the same goes for the entire rugby sevens team. Unlike those who play fifteen-a-side, we don't compete that regularly. We were told not to expect a big crowd, given how close we are to Christmas, and to focus on our games. Each family will likely send one parent, maybe a sibling or close relative, but that's it. That's more than enough for me; I don't need an audience.

On the way to the club, the pressure started building. It was wild to think that I was about to play my first official rugby games! A year ago, I was lying in a hospital bed with an IV in my arm, not even knowing this sport existed.

We arrived really early at the clubhouse, blasting a Beyoncé hit, and easily parked the small SUV in the sports complex lot. The club had called for volunteers to welcome the teams and spectators, lead site tours, manage the outdoor barbecue, and sell drinks. And who volunteered? Santi and Marie, of course. While I hurried to the locker room, they headed off to the volunteer table.

When I get to the small locker room and say hi to everyone, I notice that almost the entire B team is already there. I see

Emma talking with Claire, one of the veterans, who will play scrum-half and act as captain. She reminds me of Lucie in build—short and stocky—but far less ginger and far less pretty. She wears special protective goggles on the field because she normally wears contacts, so she's switched to the official World Rugby goggles. They make her look like a World War I pilot, which I find pretty funny. She's cool, with a high-pitched voice you can hear from far away—which is great for me, since I'll be playing on the wing. Well, "on the wing"… In rugby sevens, the winger (number 7) can just as easily cover both flanks and also act as fullback, so it's a big job that requires both speed and tackling skills as a last line of defence.

The two or three missing players arrive shortly after. I try to savour every moment because Marie told me that the locker room atmosphere before a game is unique. She's right—it's really something else, especially since you can barely hear anything over the music blasting. Some girls won't stop talking because they're so nervous and need to let it out, while others are quiet, trying to stay focused. The vibe is feverish. We're all hyping ourselves up "like crazy" (saying it actually makes me smile!)—with the sound of metal studs clicking against the floor, doors creaking and slamming open and shut at random. I breathe it all in: heat-rub, the smell of old running shoes.

Apparently, one of our players never washes her game socks out of superstition. She only changes them at the end of the season, so she doesn't jinx the team.

109

Even though I arrived mostly dressed, I've already adopted some little rituals from practice. I always do things in the same order: shorts and jersey at home; socks and cleats in the locker room, two loops and a double knot for each shoe; then, I check for my mouthguard and slip it into the mini-pocket of my shorts; finally, I look into the mirror—hair tidy, jersey tucked in neatly. Nothing should stick out. A few squats to feel the boots on my feet and break in the shorts... all good.

After the coach's talk, the minutes seem to pass more slowly. The music's still playing but not as loud. One of the girls, who's from Quebec, plays a band from back home. Apparently, it's music to win by. The veterans chat like it's no big deal; others stay quiet like me. I can feel the stress shifting gears now. I've got a knot in my stomach, I can barely breathe. Emma must have sensed it; she's been going from girl to girl, and now she walks over to me.

"Have a sip of water, breathe. Better? Now, listen to me."

She turns to the rest of the group.

"Ladies, you've already heard the coach's pep talk. In five minutes, we head out to warm up. First game is in thirty minutes. I want you all to sit down and get comfortable for a few minutes. Close your eyes. Veterans, you know the drill? The others, follow my lead, OK? Close your eyes and picture it. Make a movie in your head that's going to play out in front of your eyes. You're on the edge of the field, finishing your warm-up with short sprints, the referee blows the whistle to call our team over and check our gear."

I slip into the movie quickly—my therapist already showed me this mental visualization technique, but I'd never thought to use it for sports. The game images scroll past my closed eyelids for a few minutes. It's weird, and kind of magical. When I open my eyes at the end of the short session, I feel a little dazed, but much more focused and confident.

"Let's go! Time to warm up. Show them what you're made of!"

A burst of cheering erupts. Everyone's psyching each other up, shoulder pats and slaps on the butt. Everyone knows the warm-up routine, during which the referee talks to both captains before checking every player's equipment. As soon as we're allowed, we run onto the field and finish with starting moves. That's when I realize I underestimated the numbers— two fields, ten teams split into two pools of five, each playing on their respective field. That's ten games in total. Five in the morning, five in the afternoon. And that means around eighty players, plus coaches, assistants, physiotherapists… and family and friends. We're the home team, and there's a crowd— several hundred people now lining the edges of the fields. I tell myself, don't think about it, go into your bubble. No stress. Besides, I'm not even starting. I'm the last one in, the newbie. The game starts in a few minutes, and we huddle in a circle around Claire, who gives her captain's speech. It's my first time hearing it, and I find it inspiring, enthusiastic, and generous.

"...And don't forget, girls. You're not beginners anymore. You know better. Even if this is your first time playing sevens, most of you have already played fifteens. When in doubt, go back to what you know. And never give up. The game lasts fifteen minutes, so give it everything you've got. And if you can't go on, that's fine. We've got enough players, we'll sub you out, OK? And remember: you didn't work this hard these past few months for nothing. You've had it rough, right? So, you've earned this game! You've earned this first victory! The game doesn't start in two minutes—it's already started in your head! Are you ready?"

We shout "We're ready!" several times. I feel a surge of energy shoot through me, even though I'm heading to sit on the subs bench.

The first half goes well, but you can feel the nervous energy on the field—it's the opening game of the tournament. Unfortunately, in sevens, you only get two halves of seven minutes, so it all moves very fast. As soon as the kickoff is taken, the action is non-stop. Each team scores in turn, and since the team that scores gets to kick off again, the momentum can stretch on. The difference could come down to the conversion kicks, but nope, I'm disappointed. The kickers keep missing their drop-goals.

Some of the other subs are off doing short sprints. Emma seems to have forgotten about me. One or two have already come onto the field, and then the halftime whistle blows. Emma regroups the players for a quick talk while I hand out water bottles. The game resumes, and even though there's a lot happening on the field, I'm starting to feel a little frustrated on the sidelines. Only three minutes left. I'm desperate, but I don't dare go talk to Emma. Then she turns to me at last.

"Fatimata, you feeling fresh? Go jog up and back, do a quick sprint, and report to me. You're going in on the wing. You know what to do.|"

"Take the ball and run?"

"Exactly. And if it comes to defending, no mercy, no hesitation. Before you tackle, watch the hips. They never lie about where your opponent is going. Take her down if you get the chance. I'm counting on you."

Thirty seconds later, in a daze, I'm on the field. It's our lineout. Claire throws the ball in. Iza, our jumper, taps it down, and Claire is already in place to catch it. The back line takes off. I'm at the end of the attacking line, around midfield. I can't hear anything around me; I only see the players to my left. We're inside our own forty metres. Claire passes to Laurence, who gains a few metres and then offloads to Laura, who passes it to me chest high. A clean pass.

I'm already at full speed. When I catch the ball, I instinctively accelerate again and take off like a rocket. One defender in front of me. I fake a pass left and push into one last burst of speed. Thirty metres left to go. No one's in front of me. I don't even know what I'm doing anymore, just that once I've crossed the try line, I dive and ground the ball.

I've just scored my first try, under the posts.

Claire misses the conversion. We concede a try in return, also unconverted. At the restart, there's just time for one more play. As long as the ball stays in play and the ref doesn't blow the whistle for a mistake or obstruction, the game goes on. Victory is within reach. We regain possession, and the ball comes back to me again.

This time, I'm more aware of the sounds around me—cheers from the crowd, teammates shouting, Emma's instructions—while still keeping focused. Once again, I sprint down the sideline, outpacing the defence, and score a try in the corner.

Claire bends to pick up the ball for the conversion.

"Claire, can I take it?"

It slips out before I can stop myself. What am I doing? We lock eyes for a long moment. She sizes me up. I don't look away. I know I have the technique, the strength, and the accuracy to kick it through the posts, even from a diagonal angle on the 22-meter line.

She hands me the ball.

"All right. You scored the try—you've earned it."

"Thank you."

Emma shouts something I can't make out. I don't even turn to look. I just take the ball, line up for the drop kick... One bounce... Three steps... and—

The ball sails just inside the right post, right through the uprights!

The referee blows the final whistle. All the girls run toward me, shouting, hugging, jumping. Total joy and chaos.

I barely remember the next three games. Well, there are flashes—some moments in the spotlight, like under a "kaleidoscope" (what a great word!)—but it was like I stayed in that same dazed state. Emma quickly figured out how to get the most out of me while conserving my energy. In every game, the opposing teams seemed to discover me only after I'd scored (the "surprise effect," as coach said). One of the teams was especially tough, but we tied that game. Another was made up of tanks who hit hard; we'll have to watch out for them in the future.

In the end, we finished the tournament tied for first place, meaning the next two events will be the tiebreakers.

I was the joker from the bench—the one you send in during the second half to change the game. The day went by fast, but four games? That's a lot. Thankfully, we had fifteen players. Despite stretching between games and staying hydrated, my legs were sore. Not many tackles, but a lot of sprinting and a few tries later, I found Santi and Marie waiting for me outside the locker room.

"Bravo, sweetheart! You made the ball sing, like we used to say when I was a kid. I'm proud of you."

Marie was praising me as a player. It warmed my heart. But of course, Santi had to chime in:

"I couldn't have said it better! Oh wait, yes I could. You know the saying? When it goes to the wing, life is a beautiful thing."

"Huh?"

"OK, it means that when the ball goes out wide, so to you, we get to see some beautiful runs that end in a try!"

Lucie was with them, along with a few players from the fifteens squad. Everyone congratulated me. Pure joy. Marie and Santi agreed to let Lucie drive me home. As I stepped out of her car, she said:

"You're even more beautiful now, Nana. There's something about you—a charm I can't describe. You make me feel amazing. I want this to last."

I ended the day the same way I started it—floating on a cloud. If angels exist and walk among us, Lucie would be one of them. The last rays of sun filtered through the trees, wrapping us in a haze of warmth. Strangely, that softness suddenly reminded me of another, one laced with sorrow. A morning in Chinguetti, when joy and grief collided beneath one of the most beautiful skies I've ever seen, at least in memory. I sensed that it marked one of the saddest, most devastating days of my young life. I ran toward the house, burst through the door, and fled to my room. But even there, once I was inside, I felt the scorching heat bear down on me… and the red dust of the road sting my eyes.

CHINGUETTI, MAURITANIA, DRY SEASON 2015

Such a beautiful day. No different from the others. And yet so different. Amel is her brother, two years younger. He's coming along. She doesn't have a choice. He overheard the conversation the night before. And he always does as he pleases anyway. A bit of a spoiled child. Their younger sister is too small, so she stays home. Now, she's crying alone at the house.

The little gang sets off at dawn. It's the first day of vacation. She's finished primary school, which means she's finished school altogether. Serious life is about to begin— working with her parents, helping her grandparents, finding a husband... All the more reason to have some fun. One last time. A little escapade.

At the edge of the old village and the new town, they weave their way through part of the city, snaking between sun-dried stone buildings. Built around a central courtyard, with all rooms opening onto it. One door to the street, no windows on the outside. Centuries-old houses. Half buried. Blending into the landscape. The structures cling to the dunes, avoiding the improbable piles of creeping sand. They blend in with their surroundings by colour and material.

Farther along, one street is blocked. It's submerged in sand, which keeps advancing relentlessly. Off-limits. Only goats and donkeys still go through there. Life has nearly vanished. But they're not afraid. They keep going. They're headed to the other side of the wadi. Opposite the sand-choked *batah*. That's where the fort is. The old French fort. With square battlements.

Early morning, no tourists. It's the best time to come. To play hide-and-seek. Or war games. Barefoot, in cotton t-shirts and shorts. Boys and girls mix together, taking turns at roles. Who wants to play the French? No one. The French will climb up to the ramparts, atop the walls. The liberators stay below. The boys volunteer, of course. They'll be the ones throwing projectiles. Even if they lose in the end. The thrill of risk too. Some dare to climb the battlements.

She tried to warn him. But her brother is stubborn. He does what he wants. He runs after the older boys. He's younger, but he wants to be like them. She yelled at him. Threatened to tell their father. What else could she do? She watches him disappear around the corner of the wall, half buried in sand. She knows the place by heart. She imagines him tearing through the inner courtyard at full speed. Grabbing anything along the way that might serve as a projectile. Even small stones. It's war. Almost anything goes.

Then climbing the worn-down stairs. He doesn't look down. Even though it's high. More than five metres. But reaching the top of the rampart is more important. There, they're visible again. Barely. The dark battlements with light-coloured edges are wide, and surprisingly well-preserved. The boys are nearly unreachable. And they know it.

The attack is launched. With a chorus of screams. The assailants charge. She finds herself yelling, "Death to the French!" or "Free the country!" Objects fly through the air. A stone rips a sharper cry from her. She's hit on the arm. It hurts! The defenders believe they've won. They dance on the ramparts.

Suddenly, she sees her brother. Horror! He's climbing up the big red block. No, Amel! He tries to dance like the others. But he's only six! He loses his balance. She sees his little arms flailing. Spinning. Her mind freezes time. He seems to fall in slow motion. With a single cry.

"Nana!"

And a dull thud, barely audible. The sand softened the fall. The others have gone silent. They're frozen. Amel doesn't move either. She throws herself on his limp body. His neck is bent at an odd, unnatural angle. She's on top of him. Calling his name. Shaking him desperately.

She thinks. If her father comes, he can save him. He'll know what to do. But she has to hurry. She is oblivious to what's happening around her. One thought only: get back home. As fast as possible.

She bolts. Full speed. In front of her, her brother's smiling face. She runs breathlessly. Through sandy streets. Forbidden alleys. The old city. Narrow lanes between courtyards. With all her strength. Until she falls. Then gets up again.

In her ears, his scream. She retraces her steps. Backwards. In record time—ten minutes. She bursts through the door, screaming and crying. Her father grabs her, holds her tight by the arms. It hurts. She comes to her senses. Tells him everything.

He understands immediately. He knows the place, of course. He calls her older brother. She watches them run off.

Suddenly, she feels hollow. An emptiness inside. No strength. Depleted. She can't even think. Her mother holds her in her arms. Humming a soft melody through the tears.

Then, nothing.

TOULOUSE, MONDAY, FEBRUARY 26, 2024

Since I remembered my little brother's death, I haven't written anything. It was a shock. The holidays came and went, and my thoughts kept drifting toward Lucie… a strange mix spinning around in my head, while my piano lessons were unusually infrequent (Franck's gone travelling in the southern hemisphere). Thoughts swirl endlessly in my mind. So, I listen to rap—a lot of rap. I've also been reading extensively, mostly philosophy and poetry, Santi's latest obsession, now taking over my bedside table.

Rugby was also on pause—*la trêve des confiseurs* (the confectioners' truce) as they call the Christmas break here, a term hard to translate in Mauritania. So I ran—every day, actually, which explains the energy I feel now. Sometimes Santi joined me; he says I have *la gnaque*, real fighting spirit. I think I just needed to move, physically wear myself out, let go of all the anxiety inside me. I even told my psychologist about it, and she saw it as real progress! She's encouraged me to write in my journal more than ever.

January went by like that, with noticeably colder and wetter weather. Then came the winter break, which lived up to its name. Yesterday, a thin layer of snow covered the ground, quickly melting. "Good thing," Marie said, "otherwise, people would've panicked—we're not equipped for snow! We'd have to stay home." I nodded in agreement. I didn't want to miss going back to school after the break. But it's cold. Three degrees! I've never known that kind of cold. So I bundle up in my down jacket, my wool hat firmly in place, and my gloves ready to be put on. "Suited up for winter!" Santi declared. On the car radio, Marie had put on the group *I AM*. I love their energetic lyrics and southern French accent, and some of their melodies stick in your head long after you've heard them. We sang along during the ride, clapping along.

I thought back over the past few weeks. My memories before the crossing and the shipwreck... but not only those. I had enjoyed the break, even if it wasn't really a break for me, since I'd still gone to school throughout January. To truly catch up in all subjects and move into a regular class next year, I still needed to work hard. The goal for next year was too important: to enter *Première* and choose a major; I also wanted to get more involved in organizing a school club. I hadn't even got round to doing everything I wanted to over the holidays!

Well, I had at least squeezed in a short online Spanish course, since I want to join the Spanish club for the last term. And once again, my "free" time has been, and still is, filled with Lucie, either in thought or in person. Tonight will mark two months since we kissed for the first time.

Since then, I've actually felt more relaxed with her. Happy, even. I can say that. But I still hesitate to take that last step. She once hinted we could go further physically, and when I held back, she reassured me that she'd wait until I was ready. She hasn't brought it up again, nor asked me to sleep over. In the meantime, we do plenty of other things—here and there, sometimes rushed, often secretly. We manage to see each other at least once a week after school, like we're criminals sneaking around. Of course, it's not official. And that's not great. Deep down, I feel frustrated, maybe because I can't (or won't?) show our relationship in public. I know that, for Lucie, this isn't enough. That thought haunts me. But I hesitate, even knowing this is a natural part of a romantic relationship. I'm not ready. Something is holding me back. But what?

Wake up, Nana! Come on, get into the rhythm of the day, pull yourself together. It's back to school!

I walked through the corridor to my classroom in building D, that part of the school that feels like a labyrinth to outsiders. I know it by heart now, just force of habit, as Santi would say.

124

He calls himself a creature of habit, after all. Like, how he can eat the same cereal every morning for months. Thinking of him reminded me that I had to ask to leave class at the start of second period to meet him and Marie up at the front office. This week was Career Week at school. Every morning, we had to attend presentations by students' parents, who talked about their professions. Afterward, we'd reflect on whether we preferred an academic or professional track, like general, technical, or vocational paths. I paid close attention while Jessica, one of my two teachers, explained things. In short, it was the kind of return to school students love—light on actual work.

But what was really on my mind was what Santi and Marie would say. As professionals, their lives had collided with mine barely a year ago—and I was living proof! Would they talk about me? In what way? How would my classmates react? I'd avoided thinking about this or bringing it up with them, but now there was no getting away from it.

The first class, math, flew by. I half-listened to Jessica and worked through some geometry exercises. Later, as I walked my adoptive parents through the school halls toward the classroom, I realized it was too late to talk to them about any of my worries. I wiped my sweaty hands on my jeans and tried to muster all my strength, but despite my silent prayers, nothing came. Maybe it wasn't the end of the world—*my* world—after all? Maybe I was worrying for nothing?

I entered the classroom with a confident smile and gave a little speech to introduce Marie and Santi to the class.

It was the parents' prerogative to organize their presentations however they liked ("prerogative," such an old-fashioned word, sounds like something from the days of the musketeers). The only rule: no more than thirty minutes, including a ten-minute Q&A. Santi and Marie chose a multimedia presentation with slides, website links, short videos, and lots of photos. Santi had insisted: "Marie, let's wow them with our pictures and videos. And with these kids, you can't just talk, trust me. They need visuals, or you lose them. I heard their attention span is like 15 seconds!"

"As if you hang out with them that much!" Marie had replied with a smirk. "Other than Nana, when do you even talk to teenagers?"

That was the night before, and they had just finished everything last minute. Marie kept her tone light, not wanting to upset him. He also wanted to keep it all a surprise so I'd discover his "little gem" at the same time as everyone else. I had tried several times to sneak into the living room where they were preparing, but every time I got close, they stopped talking and closed the laptop until I left. Eventually, I gave up on their little game.

But in the end, it was more interactive and engaging than I had expected. It didn't take long for me to realize just how carefully they had prepared their presentation, far more than I had first thought. I hadn't see it coming, maybe because I was too wrapped up in my own bubble, and I found myself genuinely impressed. Santi was the first to speak, after they asked my friend Aïcha to flip a coin to see who would start. I'd heard most of his story before, but seeing him in action in front of my class—looking a little less relaxed than usual—was something else! He avoided his usual rambling, spoke in a simpler style than normal, and even used a little laser pointer to highlight the slides. A real pro!

"...After a few years of finding myself—and you're allowed to do that too, by the way—I studied international development, and got a bachelor's degree at university. Then, after graduation, I spent a year travelling around the world and doing a few internships in humanitarian aid, a great way to discover new countries. That's when I decided to work in logistics. I had discovered I could use my love of organizing things for the greater good. I did a master's degree and completed an internship at the UN, which led to a permanent position. I also benefited from contacts I had made during my international stays, especially with doctors. I eventually worked with the UN High Commissioner for Refugees, and later with Médecins Sans Frontières—Doctors Without Borders—which I'm sure you've heard of."

Two students raised their hands. He turned to the one in the back of the room.

"What's an NGO, sir?"

"An NGO is a *non-governmental organization,* basically an organization that doesn't aim to make a profit, but instead helps people. There are local ones, like food banks, and national ones, like LGBTQ advocacy groups, and international ones like MSF. You follow?"

"Yeah, thanks."

Another hand went up, no hesitation this time. I recognized the voice even in the dim light. It was Aïcha.

"Sir, I didn't quite understand. What is a logistician? You said you work on boats?"

Her question was a fair one. I remember it also took me a while to fully understand what he did on the rescue boat that saved me.

"Good question! It's not a word we hear that often. Basically, I organize the transport and supply chains for big humanitarian projects with the UNHCR and MSF. I usually have a lot of ideas, but ideas alone don't get anything done. You need resources, planning, and coordination. That's what I do. I organize the operations—contacting people, planning timelines, gathering supplies, coordinating staff on-site—often in war zones, natural disasters, or epidemics. I also oversee transportation and sometimes security. It's critical work."

Another student near the window raised her hand.

"So you don't really work on the ground?"

"You might think that. And it's true that some of my colleagues stay in the office and work by phone or online. But that's not how I do things. I go to the field to see how the plan plays out. That way I can make adjustments quickly. I really love it. Maybe that's why I've taken part in some of the biggest humanitarian operations in recent years. I'm proud to say."

Marie took over seamlessly. She looked at him with admiration, but her tone was more understated.

"Yes, Santiago is a recognized expert, and he's lucky enough to only work six months out of the year now. He's been to Haiti after the 2012 earthquake, to Liberia to fight Ebola, to war-torn cities in Afghanistan and Syria, to Somalia and South Sudan during famines, and to Asia for the Rohingya. He even worked in Central America along the migrant routes through Mexico, Guatemala, El Salvador, Honduras, and in the Mediterranean, helping refugees in rickety boats trying to reach Europe."

A low murmur of admiration spread through the room. Even I hadn't known all that, and I was honestly impressed. The teachers were scrambling to keep up, trying to pin little flags on a map of the world for each country she mentioned. It was a bit comical, though the mood wasn't light, as several students were from some of those regions. Myself included.

The emotion was tangible. Santi broke the silence with a smooth transition:

"Oh, and you were there too, weren't you? Well then, Marie, your turn! Time to tell them your story."

129

"OK, thanks. Well, I'm originally from Vietnam. I arrived with my parents when I was three, after a dangerous journey. We crossed half the globe before making it here. I was one of the last boat people who fled the Communists in the late 1970s. As far back as I can remember, even at seven or eight, I wanted to help vulnerable people, wherever they were. I did science in high school, and then studied general medicine. As soon as I finished, I joined Médecins Sans Frontières. Ten years of missions with refugees in the world's hotspots. The last five, I was the international president of MSF—less field work, more leadership. And on one of those Mediterranean rescue missions a few years ago, I had a wonderful encounter."

Phew! She didn't look at me, I thought. Then Santi chimed in, "And since then, we've always deployed together."

Then came the surprise: they presented together, just like they did in the field. It worked really well. But they never mentioned the rescue that brought me to them. Although I'd heard their stories before, this time I understood better how extraordinary their lives might seem to others. I looked around: the other students were riveted. My parents managed to finish their part in under fifteen minutes, leaving time for questions.

A hand shot up immediately.

"Excuse me, ma'am, but aren't you tired? That sounds crazy exhausting."

Good question. I thought I knew the answer, but Marie surprised me. Her reply was much more honest than the positive, optimistic things she usually said at home.

"You're right. Fifteen years of loyal service. I think I've earned a break. Let someone else young and energetic take up the torch—maybe even one of you, someday! It's so exhausting and stressful that it took me longer and longer to recover each time I came back. Honestly, I needed to settle down. The past years were filled with so many obstacles, setbacks... but also dreams and achievements. Years of fighting indifference, keeping my sense of outrage alive, trying to patch up a crumbling humanity. And now, well, it's been over six months since I've been on a mission. That's never happened since I became a doctor. I've needed the break."

Another student asked, "How many people have you saved? Have you ever counted?"

"No. Maybe hundreds? Thousands? I've never counted my patients. That might be something interesting to do if I had nothing else to do, but it's not about numbers. I'm not trying to break any records."

"And think of all the people she helped indirectly, too," Santi chimed in. "As president of MSF, for example. Here's just one example of what the organization is doing right now..."

He pulled up the MSF website. The screen filled with red dots showing where MSF was active—it was astonishing. Then he had one student choose a continent and another pick a country. He clicked on the red dot for that country, and a video popped up, showing MSF teams working on the ground. I was amazed.

Marie spoke again at the end of the clip.

"Anyway, to say I feel my duty is done wouldn't be right, given how huge the need still is. But every day reminds me what a privilege and an honour it's been to do this work. I'm proud of what we accomplished."

At that point, I had to admit I didn't understand. What she had accomplished seemed so incredible, and needing rest was understandable, but I had to ask her.

"So why stop? If you're good at it and you love it."

I couldn't help myself—it just came out like that, even though the question revealed my surprise and indignation. I hadn't even raised my hand, as if I thought I had a free pass just because they were my parents. Marc and Jessica shot me a disapproving look.

"You know, Nana, when I was your age, all that was my dream. So, I feel incredibly grateful to all the people who helped me make it happen. I've lived that dream to the fullest. But you have to know when to stop before you reach your limit. Otherwise, you break! If you were listening to what I said earlier, you should understand."

She turned to her husband, as if seeking his approval before continuing.

"It has taken a heavy toll on me, on us. You will understand maybe someday. The violence, the sickness, the despair we've been surrounded by all these years has worn us down. These are evils that wound and kill constantly. I know some of you already know this, have lived through it. Well, I often promised myself that no child would ever die again like those little ones with Ebola I held in my arms until their last breath. But that's not how it turned out. And that's not the kind of situation a human being can endure forever. Can you understand that?"

That last sentence came out with a voice thick with emotion, as if she were reliving those moments right there in front of us. She wasn't really speaking only to me anymore.

"We are deeply marked and emotionally exhausted. It's really hard on the soul," Santi added, wrapping his arms around Marie, who continued, "But there were many victories too. Collective ones. And personal ones. Like the rescue missions for refugees in the Mediterranean. Our last mission, just last year... Something changed. I can't say exactly why. Maybe it was just time to pass the torch. And now that we have a daughter, another good reason."

That's when I burst out. It was all too much for me:

"But what are you going to do now? You are important! You both are important!"

"No, sweetheart. First, no one is indispensable. And second, I've found a perfectly good replacement at MSF. So why shouldn't I take care of you now? I can also work as a pediatrician at the regional hospital—they're always in need, even here."

Santi wisely stepped in to end the mother-daughter exchange, which had gotten a little too personal. "Given you are so articulate, how about a career in politics?" Marie and I would've gone on without realizing it, no doubt—I couldn't stop myself anymore. He wrapped things up in his own original way. "Am I right, everyone? Don't you think she'd make a great politician, standing up for the downtrodden and the oppressed? Who would vote for her?"

All the students in my group raised their hands in unison. Just then, the bell rang for the lunch break—the timing couldn't have been better. I didn't much like how the conversation had ended, and I felt frustrated and sulked. Marc and Jessica congratulated Santi and Marie on their presentation, and they, in turn, thanked them for the invitation.

It was time to walk them out. We walked in silence, and just before we stepped out of the building, Santi slipped a piece of paper into my hand.

"We did a little digging. Your parents have moved. Here's their new address. Do with it what you will."

The cold hit me as I left the school, not just from the near-freezing temperature. My heart felt frozen, weighed down by that tiny piece of paper. I spent the trip back lost in distant thoughts, brooding over memories of a very different winter...

It is winter. It has never been as warm as this year, say the old folks in resignation. Not even any rain at the end of the day! It's chronic drought. She takes a sip of basil tea. Refreshing, and stronger than the evening tea. The night sounds can still be heard. It is never silent. The rustling of insects. Skittering lizards. The desert wind nearby. A few houses away, a radio is on. She recognizes the exquisite voice of Dimi Mint Abba. She inhales. Her nostrils quiver. The stubborn, slightly acrid scents of ephemeral flowers. The flowers of the desert. They last only a day. Short stem, tiny flowers, like the Maltese cross. But oh, how fragrant! From her bed, she sees the pink flowers of the *baobab chacal*. She is about to turn fourteen. Not yet menstruating. But it's coming, trust me, her mother told her one evening before going to bed. You will get them at the same age as me. That's how it is, it's heredity. Then, she will be good to marry. Generally, around her, girls marry just a little later. With a young man if it's a first marriage. With an old man, in a second or third marriage, as is her case. Her grandmother told her about the "Code of Khlil," imbued with the Sufism of their ancestors. But here, it doesn't work, the Sunnis have taken over, she whispered in her ear. This new custom allows a man to have up to four wives. Anyway, her parents have no choice. They have no more money. Her older brother is married. He's already working, and will never go to high school. Her sister is too young to bring in much. She will go to school, at least through primary. No hope for another son either. *His* shadow still lingers in the conversations. And she, at thirteen and bright, isn't she already on track to finish primary school a year early? You have enough education, her father added. They have other plans.

Her parents had no choice. They come from a lineage of Haratines, that is to say, Arab-Berbers with Negroid features. Her grandfather uses the official government nomenclature. Mimicking the Beïdanes, the "whites," the Arabs. He proudly adds: we were the first on this land, we are indigenous! But we speak an Arab-Berber language. So, officially, we are Arabs. Quite the paradox, isn't it? Then he falls back into a stubborn silence. In short, they are Haratines. Like a third of the Mauritanian population. Yet her grandparents did not follow the fate of their people. Being slaves from father to son. For reasons unknown to her—never explained—they were merchants. Like their own parents. And that long before the abolition of slavery in 1980. Then their families grew closer: their marriage was an alliance between families more than a union between individuals. Apparently, they loved each other anyway. It was the time of caravans. Long ago. The legendary desert trade routes: from Central Africa to the ocean, and even to Europe and America. Here, caravans passed through Néma, Oualata in the South, then Tichitt, of course Chinguetti, the seventh city of Islam, and Ouadane, further North. Hence her family's prosperity for several generations. But that's over. The caravans are finished, prosperity is finished, and studies are finished. Now, they are poor. Her father repeats it every day.

Already, her mother screamed and cried when they changed houses. To a much smaller house. Still traditional, with a walled courtyard and dry-stone walls. It was very small, but she remembers it. There's no question we will move to an apartment or to the big city. While I live, never! This is the last time we move! Her mother screamed, storming through the empty rooms of the new house like a tempest.

Thanks to her marriage, her parents will have money again. For a while, at least. It will be used for a business. They want to open a souvenir shop for tourists. Mohamed Ould Obeid, her future husband, promised 400,000 *ouguiyas*. Two years of an average salary! her older brother exclaimed, whistling in admiration. She knows it's eight times her mother's salary as a

137

cleaning woman. He has already given half. When she goes to him, her parents will get the other half. For the comsummation of the marriage, as they say. She does not know what that means. But it's a large sum. Mohamed Ould Obeid is a friend of her maternal grandfather. A businessman. He made his proposal properly. *Al-khoutba,* he sent his eldest son to her parents. *Al-machoura,* her parents invited their brothers and sisters for consultation. It was settled in one afternoon. No long discussion. They approved, given the circumstances. *Al-nikah,* it must be consummated—eaten?—for the marriage to be valid. It's frightening. But that is far off. Not before her menstruations. Then he will make the second payment.

She first told her father she was not ready. She was young, she could study to earn the family more money later. He corrected her. It's now we need money, not in four years. And besides, who do you think you are? A rhetorical question, as Mr. P., her primary school teacher, would say. As long as I live, it's not a woman who will make the rules for me. He continued, throwing a fierce look. Do you think we will wait for the hen that lays golden eggs, the prince charming? *Duhol mehol buri wellundu.* He dares to speak to her in Pulaar. An ethnicity they, the Haratines, usually despise. A way to insult her. But she knows the translation: better to take a simple belt than stay without pants. Choose any man rather than have none. It will always be better than remaining single. He thinks she's spoiled and capricious? Her soul and her whole body revolt. She does not need to speak. She does not lower her eyes. She dares to raise an accusatory look at her father. Well, yes, I have to make you disappear from my sight. I don't want to, but it's like that. God wills it! It's better for everyone. Even if she does not accept it, she feels pity. She understands. She knows where her duty lies. In memory of Amel. Blood for blood. She hears herself say, you will be obeyed, father. I will not shame you. If that is what pleases you.

So no fuss, no fanfare. The marriage contract is signed properly, but discreetly. No ceremony. No one wants to spend too much money. And besides, she will be his third wife. That's a lot of expenses, Nana, imagine, her mother said. Mohamed Ould Obeid was generous, he did not have to take you. You will be happy, you'll see. Do you remember what I explained? You will do as I've told you, right? You will obey. You are his servant. She replies by repeating her commands: stay clean and keep the house clean; prepare the best coffee and the best dishes; show femininity, but not too much; basically, feed the belly and the lower belly. Her grandmother adds, he must not touch you until you bleed. Your husband must treat you with respect. Like all of us. But remember, we also carry the *Kayd* in us. So it's normal that he is wary. He is afraid of you. For him, you embody revolt, disorder, evil. That is what the law says.

She moves in the next day to his house. Well, moving is not the exact word. She brings nothing. She leaves with nothing.

Just a name and an address. The gift is herself. The rest has already been given by her father. She leaves the family nest much like she left her mother's womb. Her stomach hurts, her bowels tighten at the thought of departure. She can't eat anything. What should she do? Well, take the bus, she can do that, even if it will be her first time. But after? On arrival? Will he be there? Who will welcome her? Will his other wives hate her? Will she have her own room?

The journey lasts five hours. Which seem like ten. The tin and leather heated white-hot by the sun. It's January, it's summer. The suffocating heat and animal-like closeness. Her stomachache never left her during the whole trip. Added to nausea because of the bumps. She barely glimpses the landscapes she crosses, and will never see again. The *reg* of a *hamada*, the mountain of the Zarga hills and the plain surrounded by high plateaus. She thinks only of her destination. The heat haze makes her doubt. She sees lateral lines superimposed on the horizon. A few hours later, she's there. The bus arrives in sight of the city of Atar. In the heart of the Adrar. But not her heart. For the first time, she sees Atar. Seen from afar, it is not very different from Chinguetti. Bigger, and less dirty than she thought. There are even paved roads. The bus drops her at the terminal. Forced to ask for directions, she approaches passersby. On the third attempt, someone answers.

The way is finally quite short to the address written on a scrap of paper. She did it all alone, with no one to guide her. At last. Now she stands before the high walls of the home of her husband and master, Mohamed Ould Obeid. She has not yet seen him, but she knows there will be no ceremony. No ululations, no tam-tams, no beautiful Guinea veil. No respite. No one, three, or seven days of wedding celebrations. Her childhood friends from Chinguetti are not here. Neither are her parents, her brother, or her sister. She has no one left. She is only the third wife. These ochre walls seem tall and frightening to her. Cold sweat runs down her back. She holds back tears, but she knows she will cry. No joy. There will be no pretending. And she will not pretend to want to leave, as tradition demands. She wishes she could really leave. She thinks again of her parents. Of their shop. Of their happiness. Of her little brother. Maybe even her sister will be able to go far in her studies. She must honour them. She steps toward the large double-door and lifts the metal knocker. She brings no gift. The gift is herself. A well-built, well-fed young girl, with tight, smooth, fresh skin. Still childlike hips. Breasts barely rounded, like lemons.

They approached softly; it is evening. Female voices. Now she feels hands silently pushing her. After a long corridor and an inner courtyard. Mohamed Ould Obeid's first two wives invite her to come forward, toward a green door. It is night, but here, she is about to be swallowed by another night. For her

141

whole life! At that thought, her legs tremble. She stops walking despite herself. The women take her by the arms. They carry her. A first deep, rough voice: "Come on, move, we're not going to eat you." Another younger, shrill voice: "Everyone's waiting for you for the little ceremony, hurry up." Her heart leaps: a ceremony? So her marriage is not one of those secret marriages? There is a celebration in her honour. "Have you had your period?" She answers no, not yet. Silence. Eyes narrow; she is scrutinized. Mohamed Ould Obeid will not be pleased. "Don't tell him, understood? It's impure. And forget about the ceremony! You don't want to shame your husband and master, do you? He is your *kafeel* now. He is responsible for you. And you know he's not just anyone, don't you?" She lowers her head. Better not to answer. "Mohamed Ould Obeid is the palm tree king. He owns many *zeribas* on the city's borders. If you are obedient, maybe one day you will visit them."

Meanwhile, she is led to the back of the house. A flight of stairs. Her room awaits. Much later, two eyes and a nose in the window's crack. The outline of a face. Barely a sketch. Here, through her room's opening, street smells come in. Onion and sweat too. Sometimes grilled meatballs. The braying of many goats and sheep roaming free all over the city. Children's cries. A scent of heavy, warm odors.

When Mohamed Ould Obeid comes to see her, he barely speaks. He commands, she serves. He never says anything important to her. And then, he has tried things her mother never mentioned. He is capable of doing them anywhere, as soon as they are alone. In the back of the car, in the kitchen, in the toilet, on the floor or on a sofa. Whatever place is closest if he wants to touch her. She does not know how to say no. How could she? Her mother told her he would not hurt her, as long as she obeyed. So he fondles her everywhere, presses his hands on her, slips his fingers into her intimate places. She knows he wants to put his sex inside her. But she still hasn't had her period. That moment she fears is approaching, she knows it. She has bled once or twice already. Not regularly. But thanks to that, she keeps her virtue, her purity, her worth. Then he crushes his big face against hers, breathes her all over. Noisily.

One day, his kiss changes. Softer, brushing her lips. He whispers words in her neck: "I love you, you know. You are my favourite." She feels something hard against her belly. Pushing under her white cotton pants. Her hand trembles a little when he takes it. "Trust me." He guides her hand to his lower belly and makes it move back and forth. She is surprised it is so hard. She can't think of anything else. He pulls down his pants and the thing nearly falls into her hand. It's warm. Smaller than she thought, but hard. She feels its pulse beating through those few centimetres of skin. Like a robot, she keeps going at the same pace. He strokes her back and moans. Her forearm hurts after a while.

She drifts away. She sings in her head a now familiar tune. A lament from Dimi, which Mohamed Ould Obeid does not appreciate. But women among themselves listen to their own music. Lots of Malian or Mauritanian music. Whenever she can, she stays glued to the TV. A few French shows, when she isn't helping around the house. She helps serve, helps clean, helps buy food, helps prepare meals. And so she also helps Mohamed Ould Obeid satisfy his needs as a man. He keeps telling her she is beautiful. That she will soon be his wife for good. Isn't she already? But he never explains why he puts his tongue in her mouth.

He wipes her tears tenderly. Other women often appear at that moment. They scold her: "Remember to wash yourself everywhere, at least once a day. You must be clean and ready for him." Occasionally, the phone day comes. Once a week, she can contact her parents. Fulfill her duty as a loving daughter. She tells them all is well. How could she confess the rest? They talk about the weather. Her mother always asks the same question at the end: "Did you bleed?" She wishes she could answer yes. She answers no. "May God help us!" her mother finishes.

Almost nine months have passed. The time the second wife of Mohamed Ould Obeid took to give birth. He's been indulged on one hand. But on the other, he is impatient. He phoned her parents. He still hasn't paid them the other half of what was promised. They worry. They tell him: "You are not a good husband." She can't help it. She can't explain to her mother what she must do in the meantime to satisfy him. She is too ashamed. She prefers to take refuge in music. When they leave her alone. Almost never, then. She likes Rachid Taha, for example. She would never tire of listening to him.

And one day, she wakes and her sheets are red with blood. She felt something running down her thigh during the night. A day late, like last month. She thinks she must be dreaming. There is more blood this time. She cannot hide it from the other women, and so not from Mohamed Ould Obeid. It means a big change in her life. A change she does not want. France 24 showed her these women who say no to men. She is not ready. And she does not want to be. Why? As soon as her period is over, he will visit her and hurt her with his sex. Even more. And she should be happy to get pregnant by that man three times her age? She does not want the status of full third wife. At the same time, she will finally be recognized. And her parents will be paid. They will be able to open their shop. But no, she does not want to be a good wife. It's like being a slave.

That night, he approaches like a vulture. They are in his room. He called her specifically to his room. It's the first time. It means everything. He circles her. She looks around. The luxury contrasts with what she knows. Huge four-poster bed. Massive dark wood furniture. Thick rich carpets. Suddenly, he leans toward her and kisses her with all his strength. The taste of his lips assaults her. They are still greasy from the *Maru we liham* served at supper. At once, she falls backward onto the bed. She panics. Turns her head and closes her mouth. He flattens himself on her, takes her face in his hands. Their teeth clash. Then he forces his tongue past her lips. His breath tastes of pickled onions and spices. She gags. He speaks, but she hears nothing. A distant murmur. *"Ya raya,"* she prefers the music playing in her head.

Mohamed Ould Obeid's embrace is passionate. Prisoner of his weight, she stops moving. He lifts her dress. Now, he writhes. She cannot speak. He stuffs his tongue in her ear. He orders her: "I don't want to see your teeth. Close your eyes." One last look to realize his eyes are burning. She closes hers and lets her mind drift. She goes far away. She is a wild animal freed. An almost impossible-to-catch beast. A long, slim snake slithering fast and high. She feels Mohamed Ould Obeid moving on her. Another woman would feel that, but she feels nothing. She would like to say something beautiful. Something grandiose: Husband, let me caress you. My caresses are softer than honey. Let me enjoy your generous beauty. And, thanks to me, you will have a great destiny.

But her leading the lovemaking is just a dream. He penetrates her by force. He plants his devastating blade. The music continues. The snake is pierced, cut in two. It no longer bothers her. She slips over the sand without leaving a trace. Afterwards, there is just a slight burning with every thrust of his hips. Fortunately, the act lasts only as long as the song. At once, she even surprises herself by wanting to bite him. To bite him while losing her virginity. And to bite him again. On the face, on the sex. An eye for an eye, a tooth for a tooth. She is about to do it but pulls back. As he withdraws, she feels tears on her cheeks. Warm and salty, running into her mouth and down her neck. He whispers: "Thank you, Nana, that was very good." The music gives way to silence. She sobs. He gets out of bed, pulls up his pants, and shows her the door. He goes toward an adjoining bathroom to wash. Without looking back.

The other two wives appear instantly. They congratulate her. According to them, she is now a woman. And before, what was she? She realizes she aches all over. Taking small steps, she lets herself be led to the large perfumed bath, where she stays for an incalculable time. Like a very sick person. It is her privilege on the wedding night. Shaking, she then curls up and sleeps in her cold bed. She will remember that night for a long time. A night of nightmares. And dreams. She thinks again of those women on TV shows on France 24. They dare sometimes to push men away; they call them primitive. They pity them but do not yield. Part of her admires those women. To hell with a husband's protection! To hell with the strange relief of knowing one is safe! What safety? What protection? He is her first tormentor. She still recalls her mother's words: Once you are with your husband, you will fear nothing anymore. But what if it were the opposite for the rest of her life? That is the night she makes her decision.

TOULOUSE, SUNDAY, MARCH 10, 2024

Since my last recollection, I have realized quite a few things. At the moment, these very painful memories just paralyzed me, and it's thanks to the encouragement of Santi and Marie that I found the strength to share them with the psychologist. As she says, it doesn't solve everything; it's just one step on the road to recovery. I have music, books, rugby and friends to support me as well. And I also don't believe things will get better immediately, because all this information that surfaces brings with it intense emotions and more questions than answers. So, as a result, I accepted that an attempt at contact be made because I want to know what happened afterward. Will my parents get my message? Did Mohamed Ould Obeid take revenge for my running way? Did they open the business of their dreams? What has become of my older brother, my little sister, and my grandparents? Do they know that I'm alive? Do I still exist in their eyes?

Besides that, practices all winter have been fruitful, and the women's rugby sevens team is more united than ever. We no longer feel like a B team. We've all gained confidence in our rugby, and the wins at the first tournament definitely helped a lot. The prospect of playing the same teams again no longer scares us. We're confident we can face them. As for me, I'm running more than ever from one activity to another. I started Spanish club during the week, and even without Saturday games, I barely find time to settle in my room, which has become more of a transit zone. I feel on fire and a bit tense too, but good in my body, fully in control of myself. My ongoing assessment results seemed generally as good as the first term so far, and now the more important end-of-term exams are coming. I was counting on my regular class work so I wouldn't have to study too much for those exams. Anyway, I wasn't sure I would have the time, especially because all the French Model United Nations clubs had to meet one last time shortly after the second tournament, this time in Paris. All deadlines were arriving at once, but I managed. The next two weekends would therefore be very busy. After that, most of my remaining personal time was devoted to Lucie.

As the club's bus exited the highway, I was suddenly thrown forward, my head knocking against the seat in front of me. Our 200-kilometre bus trip was coming to an end. We were arriving in Perpignan for the long-awaited second tournament. As I rubbed my forehead and adjusted my earphones, Dobacaracol kept playing. Another music suggestion from Santi and Marie that I really like, and which helped me dive back into thoughts of Lucie and our last meeting. She is my girlfriend, hidden from the world's eyes, since neither of us told our parents, and we don't let people know we are a couple at school. Lucie, with her slightly chubby face, her green, laughing eyes, her breasts, her round and muscular buttocks. Lucie, with her thick, fragrant hair. Once again, all the surrounding noises drifted away, pushed into the background. I closed my eyes and pictured us last night, on a bench behind a thicket, deep in a park overlooking the city. It's one of our city refuges, where we're never disturbed. Sitting quietly at first, only our thighs touched. She's in jean shorts and I'm in a summer dress. Our clothes weren't really suited for this still chilly March, not quite spring yet, but they allowed skin-to-skin contact that electrified us. At one point, we turned to face each other at the same time. Our gazes met, the fire smouldered. I got goosebumps just thinking about it. I still feel my lashes flutter with emotion, my pupils dilate. Our eyes moved slowly closer. I could hear her breathing and catch the fruit-sweet scent that lingered on her lips. Our mouths drifted apart, then found each other again. On my tongue and in my nostrils remains the sweet scent of her neck. Soon, our hands begin to wander, our movements urgent. I was overcome by a terrible heat. Then Lucie gently guided my hand, which had been caressing her breasts, down beneath her shorts, between her thighs, and…

"Ladies, we've arrived! Gather your bags and trash. Please don't leave anything behind, even if we're taking the same bus back. Check that you haven't forgotten any equipment…"

The wake-up was brutal… and frustrating. For a few seconds, I felt like I could still smell her intoxicating perfume. A bit disoriented, I looked around; the other players had already put on their club jackets. All were standing, some waiting in the central aisle to get off.

Our first opponents this morning are the only team that beat us at the first tournament. And this time, the Perpignan girls are playing on their home turf! Luckily, we're ready enough to meet their challenge, but we'll have to get into the game from the very first second. To start, and for me personally, the ritual is important—that is, attention to small gestures that help focus. So I first go to the bathroom to put on my shorts and jersey, then come back with the others to the locker room, where I put on my socks and cleats. Two wraps of laces around each shoe and a double knot later, I'm almost ready. I check that I have my mouthguard, which I put in the small pocket of my shorts, my bottle filled with a rehydration drink, and a cereal bar. In front of the mirror, I finish with a final hair check and a double-check that my jersey is properly tucked into my shorts. All good, I'm ready for the mental visualization exercise Emma showed us at the first tournament. We go straight into warm-up after that, and with a lot of focus, we're ready to fight.

Thirty minutes later, the game started, but I'm still on the bench as a substitute. Like last time, our opponents are quick and good with their hands—no dropped balls, no forward passes. But we've prepared well, and our tackles are flawless. At the end of the first half, we're behind by just one try, five small points. We have an obvious problem though: they're always outnumbering us when they have the ball. They systematically double up after each pass, quickly over-whelming us. On top of that, they are able to execute every kind of pass—cross pass, inside, outside, skip pass—with such skill that we can't keep track of what's happening. As a result, two converted tries back-to-back really hurt us.

At Emma's insistence, I go back in at the start of the second half. We have possession at the kickoff, and the scene from my first game flashes through my mind. I position myself exactly as I did then to receive the ball, and when Laura sends it my way, I do what I always do. I'm confident now. I haven't dropped a pass in a while, not even under pressure. Once the ball is in my hands, I pick up speed again, relying on my sprinting ability and solid footing to change direction if needed.

But something feels off. I sense someone closing in behind me…fast. A second later, someone grabs my jersey from behind, pulls me back, and wraps me up—taking me down.

Instinctively, I roll as I hit the ground. It's my first serious tackle from behind in competition, and the shock of it makes me drop the ball. Knock-on! My tackler is already back on her feet and snatches the ball. She plays the advantage while I'm still on the ground. By the time I get back up, they've scored again.

Two minutes later, I find myself facing Perpignan's last line of defence inside their 22. I pull off the best sidestep and swerve of my life, accelerating like a rocket—I think I've beaten her... But she grabs me, tears the ball from my hands, and bolts. An eighty-metre sprint later, they've scored again. Once more, the shock paralyzes me.

We take advantage of the one-hour break before the next game to take stock because all the girls seem a bit dazed, like me. Instead of blaming each other and looking for scapegoats, Emma invites us to return to basics: hydration, snacks, stretching, and feedback, where everyone gets to speak and vent; Emma speaks last. Several of us admit our mistakes, saying we're not fast enough, not adaptive enough, too eager to score... In short, each of us finds a flaw.

"Shake it off. The flies will land somewhere else soon enough. The problem, girls, is that you played just as well as the first time," Emma says.

"Huh???"

"But not them. They played even better; they improved so much in several areas of the game! The three months of

153

practice paid off. And for you? You can take them as a model for your next game. One detail: they didn't try a single high kick or follow-up kick. No cross kicks either. That's a weakness. We could try, we have some good kickers. That said, they didn't need those to get through our defence. Think about that and come back ready to give 100% for the second game."

No one says anything. No shouts, no cheers, no little group dance, and I am beginning to feel like I don't deserve a place on the team. The coach didn't even speak about my role in the loss, like she didn't expect much of me anyway. True, I ran as fast as I could, but I lost the only two balls I got, and we conceded a try each time.

Santi and Marie came over to support me. I take five minutes to speak with them, but my heart's not in it. They know I need to be alone because it's up to me to find part of the solution, even if we'll solve our problems collectively. I find a quiet corner, away from the playing fields, where I can lie down in the shade and close my eyes. What more can I do, or what can I do differently?

Fifteen minutes later, Rachida comes to get me, and we head back into the fray. I hope I'll have a few answers to offer my teammates. In any case, I haven't wasted my time during that break. Fortunately, for this second game, our opponents are real blocks—just as wide as they are tall—but slower than us. Too heavy to outrun us, they were also very clumsy handling the ball back in December, and this gave us opportunities to capitalize on their many knock-ons. And since scrums are simplified in rugby sevens, with just a single line of three players, they couldn't even use that to their advantage. It had cost them the win. The game kicks off under a threatening sky, and a thunderstorm could break at any moment, putting an end to the game immediately. The team of colossuses, as I call them, looks much like the one we already beat—no new players at first glance. But in the opening minutes, surprise: their defence plays extremely high and aggressively. They come up on us much faster than expected when we're on the offensive. And their tackles hurt. They play dirty, literally falling on top of us in the tackle.

When they have the ball, same story. They've understood that their weight and size make them hard to stop. Even without speed, they advance, and we're forced to bend excessively to tackle them low. Laura, our inside centre, pays dearly for her middling tackling technique: poorly positioned on a slightly high tackle, she flips her opponent onto herself, and I see her completely crushed for a few seconds under the brute. She doesn't get up right away, then asks to be subbed off —she's already showing signs of a concussion. Emma asks me to take her place. I promise myself to tackle as safely as possible. But I can't avoid contact, and they're locking us down too well on attack. There are only a few seconds left in the first half—we're once again trailing by five points. Coming out of a ruck, Claire, the scrum-half, tries to catch them off guard by, instead of passing, taking off solo with the ball—the prerogative of a scrum-half. Unfortunately, they've expected this, tackling her immediately. But she manages to pop the ball away just in time. On defence, they're simply much better positioned. That's when I realize this is how they make up for their lack of speed—they can't afford to give up too much space. So we have to play wide, doubling up or using skip passes, beating them at their own game and outflanking them!

I don't even have time to shout my thoughts to the other girls before a monstrous player ferociously tackles Claire, lifting her up, before our stunned eyes, and flipping her over like a pancake—head down! It's a textbook "spear tackle"! I'd never seen anything like it, except in those banned videos the coaches warned us about, with a serious look: "That's not rugby."

As she hit the ground, her neck made a strange noise, and she screamed in pain. The ref blew her whistle right away and ran to Claire, pulling out a red card, and stopped in front of the offender, yelling at her. On the sideline, Emma was also screaming, swearing at the player and her coach with every name in the book. The game was halted while we waited for medics. Claire was immobilized immediately because she couldn't feel her neck, and evacuated by ambulance thirty minutes later. The game didn't even last a half, and under the rules, the remaining seven minutes would not be replayed.

Except for Emma, who stayed with Claire the whole time, the rest of us gathered on our side of the field, not really knowing what to do. Some parents, including Santi and Marie, came to get us and bring us to the barbecue area. We had to eat something before our third game of the afternoon, though no one was really in the mood.

As we nibble, emotions explode—tears, shouting. Everyone is traumatized, and I can't stop picturing Claire on the stretcher in her neck brace... but over her face I see Lucie's. The image of that spear tackle replays in my mind endlessly—I can't focus on anything else. How are we going to continue playing? I search for ideas, words to say, some source of motivation. Lucie whispers in my ear—someone has to get a grip, speak up, rally the team, or it'll be a disaster. "Nana, do something—think of your teammates, your coach, the parents who came all this way, think of Claire." It's up to me to honour everything I've learned these past months: we don't back down from the opposition, we face them head on!

"OK, girls, come here! Let's pull ourselves together. You've had half an hour to recover, eat and digest. Now, let's warm up again. Clear your mind of anything unrelated to this game. Close your eyes, picture yourselves jogging around the field to warm up, then..."

I went on, repeating phrases I'd heard a hundred times from Emma or the team psychologist. After a few minutes of visualization, I looked around—every player seemed more determined, a little calmer. The fear I felt when I saw Claire assaulted had turned into a rage I needed to unleash immediately.

"We have to do something, girls! Claire's in the hospital, Laura's gone home—we can still honour them. Show them we won't give up, that we'll fight to the end."

"You're right, Nana. I couldn't have said it better. Play your rugby! Give it your all. For your teammates! That's all that matters now. I'm not even talking about winning. Who cares? Just go out there and have fun! But don't let anything get by. That's rugby spirit too. Let's do a jog around the field, then back to warm-up routine. Let's go, ladies! Nana, can I talk to you?"

Emma had come back without me noticing—it was she who had picked up where my little speech had left off. What did she want? I feared the worst—I'd taken an initiative I wasn't supposed to…

"Nana, I want to try you as scrum-half. You've gained confidence, and you're able to take initiative. You just proved that. If we're blocked on attack, like last game, you'll know how to kick to get around the defence. You've developed a great reading of the game. Combine that with your burst of speed, it could work. You also know the girls well enough now. Are you up for it?"

At that moment, I think hard about Orelsan's rap. But I don't hesitate a second. I dream of no longer being just the runner who catches the ball and sprints, but someone who makes tactical decisions in the heart of the action. A few minutes later, a storm breaks out. After thunder and lightning, and with a bit of delay, the game starts. And it's in a torrential downpour, in a strange state of collective fury. Not the usual nervousness, but more like rugby-crazed warriors. We were everywhere—on every ball, at every moment. Eager to keep or regain possession, we made a record number of technical errors, giving our not-so-skilled opponents plenty of chances to win the ball back through penalties. So, yes, there was a lot of waste, but simply put, we wanted it more than they did. My poor passes coming out of scrums and rucks, our failure to throw the ball in properly at lineouts, didn't stop us from scoring several tries. And without realizing it, we burn through almost all our remaining energy in this game. Yet we still have one more game to play in our five-team pool, as in all regular season tournaments.

Once again, Emma entrusts me with the captaincy and the number 4 position, but it's a disaster! This time, my opposite number sticks to me the entire game, even during ball exits, where I constantly feel her on my heels. I even end up dropping the ball under her tackles after scrums more than a few times. Despite everything, I try to vary my moves, especially with different choices—passing, kicking, keeping the ball—and switching left/right, but with little success due to a lack of precision. My passes are often too low, my clearance kicks go straight into touch—in short, my performance is disappointing.

In my case, the problem can't just be fatigue, just as with my teammates, but our lack of collective resilience is too obvious. Some players don't even run anymore, not even the substitutes, and we were twelve without the two injured players! Oh! And to top it off, we now have another injury: Rachida, our jumper, suffers an ankle sprain after a bad landing from a line-out jump. We've just lost a fifth of our squad in a matter of hours —this is unheard of! The score is almost secondary at this point, but we didn't even score. 33 to 0, the worst result of our season, and we drop to third place in the rankings. Before heading off to change and leave, Emma still gathered us in a circle.

"Ladies, you're down, soaked, you're cold, and we have three injured. By the way, Claire is doing okay. It's a neck sprain. It'll take several months, but she'll recover. She'll be back at the end of the season. So it's more fear than harm. And we'll visit her at the hospital next week. I'm sorry this tournament ended like this. It happens, the harsh return to reality in sport for you. I understand. So now isn't the best time for big speeches or "feedback." We'll do that next week, at practice. Until then, reflect on your playing. Everyone has things to work on. Learn from your opponents—their good plays, their good technique. Think it over and digest all of it. I've confidence in you, and we'll bounce back."

I got the message, and in that moment, I thought it was meant for me, maybe just a feeling. On top of everything, my mind was in a fog I was so deeply shaken. There was just too much in my life, too many ingredients in an overly complicated recipe. Work was waiting for me—in every sense of the word —personal, school-related, and rugby-related. What time could I still give to Lucie, whom I thought was the centre of my universe, alongside Santi and Marie? I spent the entire return trip all worked up, a restless half-sleep that wasn't restful at all. "I'm afraid of failure" looping in my headphones. I kept wondering if we hadn't just been too cocky going into the tournament. Getting off the bus, even before going home or showering, I felt completely drained. That rugby Sunday was a real nightmare.

TOULOUSE, THURSDAY, APRIL 4, 2024

This Thursday wasn't an exceptional day—not even the first day of spring—yet the atmosphere at school had changed. A kind of joy, good cheer, was in the air from the start of classes. The cold and dampness that had lasted for months had vanished, and the temperatures were warming up. Suddenly, it seemed like shorts had invaded the hallways—and so had the shouting. A general excitement spread through the classrooms. A contagious enthusiasm seemed to touch even the most barren hearts... or the heaviest ones, like several members of the team who still hadn't digested the results of the last tournament.

As for me, I like this abrupt shift. I want to turn the page on my losses and injuries. This year, I want to savour the upheaval, the almost physical jolt that it brings. Suddenly, conversations are flooded with words like "beach," "weekend," or for some, "hot spots," "kite-surfing." I welcome the change —even for me, the sea now has a completely different meaning. But maybe it's not wholly positive, because I grew up inland and open water is still a dangerous and exotic element. Sometimes, just thinking about it brings back memories of my escape to Europe, and I feel sick.

All day long, I genuinely admired this momentum toward pleasure and happiness, but from a distance, from the outside looking in. All the more because if I'm still at school this late today, it's because my adoptive parents had been called in. It's the second round of parent-teacher meetings, the one that comes with the second term report card, by invitation only, meaning for students in difficulty.

My good mood had quickly vanished when I heard about the meeting, and today, it's a nightmare. After a few polite phrases, sitting around a round table reserved for meetings in one corner of our classroom, Santi, Marie, and my two teachers get straight to the point. Jessica speaks first.

"Apart from French and English, where Nana's made great progress, her results have mostly failed to improve this term, and even dropped in science and math. More importantly, we've noticed she seems physically tired and clearly less enthusiastic in class."

Santi responds quickly.

"Look, we're really surprised. This has never happened before since she started classes last year—first online, then here at the high school. She's always been making progress. And she worked really hard over the holidays to keep up."

Marie jumps in, sounding worried.

"As for the tiredness, we've noticed that too. She has two official rugby practices with the club, but she's also added some speed training—with you, Marc. She even decided to join a Spanish club a few lunchtimes a week, just for fun. We encouraged her to do so. She loves languages. And you know she goes jogging every day on top of rugby—forty-five minutes of running, either early morning or late at night. There's also piano, and the weekly therapy sessions have brought up some difficult and disturbing memories."

"Listening to what you've just said, don't you think this might all be a little too much for her, both physically and mentally, and that the heavy load of classes, activities, and training could actually be starting to wear her down?"

I sit there feeling helpless and extremely uneasy at being blamed. So, I go quiet—that's something I'm good at. They haven't mentioned my time with Lucie, but I start to think about it.

Marie jumps back in.

"I get the feeling there's more to it. What happened at the last rugby tournament, Nana?"

Are they talking to me? My mind was already somewhere else... with Lucie.

"Well, we lost more games than expected. Three out of four, actually. And ended up in third place."

"That's all?"

"That's already a lot."

"No, I mean, how'd you feel about that day, like, personally?"

"Not great. I didn't run well—like, the other teams were totally ready for me. I got tackled way too much. I wasn't hurt or anything, but I didn't play how I wanted, and it kinda messed the whole team up. Plus, our scrum-half, Claire, got slammed by a spear tackle. She had to go off in an ambulance. I stepped in for her, but I didn't do a great job."

"A spear tackle?" Jessica asks.

"She was grabbed, lifted vertically, and flipped head down!"

I mime the motion to be more clear. The teachers and even Santi grimace.

"That's very dangerous and completely illegal," Marie adds.

"I think for a moment, I thought it was Lucie, my best friend, on the stretcher. It was like watching her die. I was terrified, I panicked. Lucie and Claire look so alike."

The adults are silent for a few seconds, processing what I just said. Could that really be what made me lose my desire to play? Well, no, I haven't exactly lost it. At practice, I still give 100%, happily. Okay, I have to push myself a bit for the extra speed sessions. And things with Lucie are going well. Except that our relationship isn't official, which bothers me more and more, maybe even more than it bothers her. I try not to think too much about it and the months ahead, so not to be too disappointed if things end between us.

Marc speaks.

"You adopted Fatimata last year, didn't you?"

"Actually, it's been a bit longer now. Things were finalized a little less than two years ago." Santi answered.

Bringing that up now was a bit surprising. What's the connection? I asked myself.

"Do you mind if we talk about it?"

"We've been clear from the start. Yes, it was a late adoption, but it was something we all wanted. Nana wanted it too, if that's what you're asking."

"No, that's not it. Nana, did you lose your parents?"

"Uh, yeah, well… sort of. Let's just say I lost contact with them years ago. And they're far away, in Mauritania. Actually, we're waiting for news, because Marie and Santi recently offered to reach out to them again. But I think… I'm afraid… I'm probably dead to them!"

The moment I say those words, I realize how horrible they sound. Really horrible to think that my parents, having had no news of me for two years, might believe I'm dead. Tears stream down my cheeks, and I collapse into Santi and Marie's arms.

The meeting ends not long after. I'm in a daze, barely catching the teachers saying they'll sign me up for after-school tutoring. Once we're back home and I start coming out of the fog, Santi calmly explains everything. The changes will be easier to manage since one time slot is free now—the Model UN club has ended, as scheduled. Spanish is also done for me this year—we'll see about next year. And jogging is also off the table, except in gym class, but the sprint training with Marc will continue once a week. Apparently, no one brought up my relationship with Lucie, which is a relief, though part of me wishes we'd just settle things once and for all.

We'll see if this new setup helps. But something's got to give. I've realized I'm at my breaking point. Deep down, I know these measures are only part of the answer and just a temporary fix. The nightmare isn't over. I'm rock bottom, and I have to look up and try to catch a glimpse of sky. Suddenly, I imagine my father, my mother, my brothers and sisters reaching out to me.

For Santi and Marie, I'm their only, their one and only child, but back in Mauritania... Even though I was just a girl and middle child there, somehow I can't stop thinking about those days, like my brother's wedding, when everything felt happy.

TOULOUSE, THURSDAY, APRIL 18, 2024

"No, no, and no! Start your acceleration lower and tighter! Lift your knees, use your arms! Increase your pace, shorten your strides for the first few metres! That way, you'll be more powerful on impact if an opponent gets in your way."

I stepped away once again to return to my starting position on the edge of the field; I had been going back and forth across the width of the field for twenty minutes. A short "quality" training session that was turning into a "nightmare," a word I'd been using far too often lately. I lay down on my stomach once again, nose in the grass, waiting for the start signal.

"On your mark! Ready! Set! Go!"

I was doing my best, but it wasn't working. I wasn't running fast enough. The prone position was supposed to force me to launch my body forward, a way to get a quicker start.

And I *had* improved over the past few weeks… for the first few metres.

"No, no! Coordinate your movements! You need to open up after the first ten metres, lengthen your strides. Swing your arms! No need to breathe at the beginning. After that, let it all go. Otherwise, you'll never hit your peak. Come on, you can do better."

That, too, I'd been hearing a lot lately… I got back into position. Tiny black dots floated in my field of vision, superimposed on the scenery. The sun was still beating down, and Marc, my coach, was nothing but a shadow. Squinting, I could read the disappointment on his face. After all, *I* had asked him to coach me because I'd heard he used to do track and field. And he still did triathlons—he was a runner, so to me, the best person to help. He was training me on his own time, so I owed him some real effort. I returned to the starting line, focusing on carefully applying everything he'd told me, even though my lungs were burning. I couldn't catch my breath, but it didn't matter—I had to push through! Every movement, one by one, broken down step by step. My footing was good. It was everything else that needed work. I had to hang in there.

"On your mark! Ready! Set! Go!" And I was off again.

As I was about to start my third acceleration, just twenty metres to go, a sharp pain sliced across my stomach.

"Ayy, yerr! I can't…!"

"What's wrong Are you okay?"

"It hurts. A sharp, stabbing pain just under my ribs."

"Only there? Anything else?"

"I can't breathe. I've never hurt like this before! I'm done for today."

I was doubled over in pain. Did he think I was faking it? My mind completely overwhelmed by the pain, I didn't even say goodbye. I went home angry. In my ears, the words of an Angèle song were rewinding, and I was more frustrated than anything else. As I walked, the pain seemed to lessen a little. I was able to recall what Emma had said to me after the first practice following the "historic" Sunday of the second tournament. She had insisted on speaking to me privately.

"Despite the losses, I stand by what I said to you last Sunday. You've become a more rounded player, you've developed real confidence in your technique and your potential. You've also gained excellent endurance. But stepping in last minute for such a crucial position like scrum-half put you in a really tough spot, with a lot of pressure. I don't want you to beat yourself up too much about that, okay?"

"But I *felt* ready! And I wanted it!"

"That doesn't mean you were ready. So, I take my share of responsibility. The problem is your acceleration at the start just isn't strong enough."

"Uh, I'm not sure I follow. It's true I had trouble breaking away from the number four on the other team in the last two games."

"When you get into your run, you do really well. Your top speed is excellent, although you could improve your footwork and your balance in changing direction. But I really think the main thing is your start."

"What can I do?"

"You need to do targeted training, like a 100-metre sprinter, to make your start more powerful. That will also help with your acceleration phases."

"Oh! So there are *phases* of acceleration too? I think our phys ed teacher mentioned that. We're just now starting a track and field unit."

"Is your teacher trained in that area?"

"Well, he does triathlons. He can certainly run. I'll ask him."

"Go all in on this. Use the opportunity to build muscle in your thighs. You'll see the difference."

"Okay, thanks, coach."

"One last thing. Starting next week, if you want, you're cleared to train with the fifteen-a-side squad."

"You mean I'm back on Team A?"

"Exactly. In a few weeks, you'll be playing your first 15-a-side rugby game, on the wing."

Now, after that training session that ended in a dog's breakfast (nice image, right?), everything was going down the drain (Get it? Ha, ha!). I had to make sure I didn't get hurt again! But my bad luck just seemed to go on. What else was heading my way? Should I stop running altogether? And rugby? Or maybe it wasn't an injury, just a huge side stitch. I arrived home completely wrecked, half bent over—I really felt like someone was stabbing me in the belly. It was worse than period pain! I went up to my room without saying a word so I wouldn't alarm Santi or Marie, but I'd barely lain down when I heard a knock at my door.

"Sweetie… Nana, are you okay? Can I come in?"

I tried to unclench my jaw to answer.

"Yes, of course."

"How did training with Marc go?"

I couldn't pretend anymore.

"Not great, actually. My stomach hurts, here on this side." I lifted my T-shirt to show her.

"Hmm, it looks a bit swollen, doesn't it? Did it come on suddenly?"

"Not really. I don't remember exactly. But I've been getting side stitches lately, always in the same spot. And I've been running less, since I cut back on jogging, but it's happened two or three times during rugby practice. I don't think that's the cause. Or maybe I'm just out of shape."

"You really should have told me sooner! May I examine you? I don't think it's a side stitch or a simple injury."

The next morning, Marie told me I had an appointment at the hospital the following Monday. They needed to remove my appendix. In three days! I also learned that this little organ is useless but can become painfully inflamed and degenerate into "peritonitis," a word that sounds like a mineral but actually is an inflammation, which causes intense pain and can kill you. Since the inflammation was acute, they weren't going to take any risks. Marie reassured me a little: it was a routine, benign operation—I'd only be in the hospital for a day. The rest of the week I'd spend in bed at home, which meant all training was cancelled for a while.

I guess I just had to deal with it and wait at least two weeks before I could even think about working out again. I was really bummed out. It honestly felt like my whole season was over. And if that was true, then seriously, what was even the point? But I've always been good at running, like, for as long as I can remember, and nothing had ever stopped me before. My thoughts began to drift—the situation had unexpectedly stirred up other memories. I was in shock, even if being surrounded by Santi, Marie, and Lucie was comforting. I was about to text Lucie, but instead, I just let all those memories come back, like I was slipping into the cool stillness of a *guelta* in the middle of a blazing summer afternoon.

Chinguetti, Dry Season 2018

She has always loved to run. Though she's never seen a gazelle, her father often compares her to one. In the streets of Chinguetti, she is the queen of running. When all the children play tag, she's usually the last to get caught. When they play soccer, no one can stop her, except with a good shoulder check. But she's not afraid. In fact, she likes the contact.

She sometimes hears the boys talking among themselves. They call her a "tomboy." Sometimes they even look at her with a bit of fear. She knows why. And she's proud of it. What does it change? She's a girl. And she knows how to head the ball. She's not afraid her headscarf will fall off. The secret is to tie it well from the start. They don't know that. And anyway, she's proud of her long hair too. Of her round features. Of the smoothness of her skin over her taut frame. Of her long legs.

Her grandmother talks to people about her face, with her doe-like eyes and long eyelashes. And even if she's not very tall, she's a beautiful girl. Or so she believes. They've been feeding her well lately. Her parents insist on it.

She plays a lot with the boys. All kinds of games, at all times. Usually in the street. Especially after school. Among the beautiful houses with blue or green doors and window frames of the old town. Among the mud-brick houses rising from the dunes.

But you still have to be careful. Step aside when the police car or the new bush ambulance speeds past. Otherwise, it's quiet—the street belongs to them. Sometimes a melody drifts out from a doorway and accompanies their wild dash. They weave between passersby. People walk a lot in Chinguetti. Either they're too poor to have anything but their legs to get around. Or they're tourists. You can tell them by their light skin. They come and go depending on the year. It all depends on the war, on the armed groups.

This year, the tour operators have put Chinguetti back in their brochures. So now, you see quite a few white people in "Saharan" outfits, in what they call "colonial" shorts. They like walking in the dust, breathing in the dust. Because they don't live here.

That ochre dust that seeps into her very skin—she sometimes gets sick of it. Especially in spring, when the wind blows all the time. "Zero visibility!" as her father says.

The children swarm around the tourists like flies swarm around them. They greet them with "Nazrati! Nazrati!" They often ask: "Are you really Moorish, little one?"

It's her dark copper skin that makes them say that. Not quite black, but certainly not light-skinned. Not *Beïdhanie*, but *Haratine*. But they wouldn't understand the nuance.

They're not nomads. Her family has been here longer than her grandmother can remember. They have a solid house. It needs to be raised every two or three years, but still.

The visitors want to see the desert and the old houses. Even if half of them are sinking further into the landscape. The sand is taking over. They want to admire the remains of the seventh-holiest city of Islam.

The desert is winning. And as for the desert, it's simple. They live in it. Chinguetti *is* the desert, in every sense.

But let's admit it: some of the drawings on the walls are truly beautiful. "They're *rupestre* paintings," her grandmother declares with a scholarly tone. She guesses that "*rupestre*" means "very old." So, respect. You mustn't touch them.

She continues. If you touch the drawings, you'll wake up the microorganisms that have been sleeping there for millennia. And once awakened, they'll eat them. That's why they spray and calcify them.

She runs to get home before nightfall. A few drops hit her head. Though it rains very little. The elders complain, blame it on the young, their farming methods, the near-permanent war. So many words. She nods. It's already over.

She bursts into the house. She runs to her room to look up those new words. From a big metal biscuit tin, she pulls out her French dictionary. An old, yellowing Robert with a loose binding. She loves words. For as long as she can remember.

She's always lived surrounded by books. "We don't have money, but we have books," her grandfather says. Old books, in old boxes. They're never taken out. "They're our treasure. The family inheritance. We'll never sell them," her father regularly declares, scandalized at the thought.

Her grandfather adds solemnly: "We may have the smallest libraries, but they're the most beautiful in Africa!"

Of course, she's curious. She's opened a few of the books. Qur'an and hadiths, but also philosophy, mathematics, astronomy, history, and literature. At first, she doesn't understand anything. But like the rock paintings, she understands that they're beautiful. The drawn letters (calligraphy), the illustrations. In Arabic. She's been studying Arabic since second grade, but it's still very hard. The books' goatskin covers still carry a scent, a funny one. And the parchment pages crackle. "Only the elders may touch them," her mother warns.

So she prefers to dive into her parents' books. Pocket editions in French. Children's classics. Novels and poetry collections from the time when they could still afford to buy them. She doesn't understand everything. Sometimes she skips pages. One day, she tells herself she really must make an effort to improve her French. Just for this.

I knew it, I knew this day would come! Already, at the start of the school year, I remember having mixed emotions (excitement, but mostly fear) when I realized I'd be taking art classes. Having the chance to create with words and images, learning to draw, paint, sculpt, play music, dance—all of that was so new! My fear didn't come from that: I was really happy and excited to start, as long as there wouldn't be any public performance.

The first term was devoted to drawing and painting, which ended with an exhibition at the school library—perfectly fine by me. Apart from the official launch evening, where all students from the integration class were obviously expected to attend, I never had to appear in public. And even then, hidden in the hubbub and the crowd, I went practically unnoticed.

In the second term, music was the focus, which couldn't have made me happier. No need to say that I found the introduction to the different instrument families—brass, percussion, woodwinds, strings...—incredibly enriching. We got to try everything! On top of my piano lessons with François, each of my two weekly sessions was pure delight. We even got to choose an instrument at the end and perform a short piece from those selected and offered by Marc and Jessica. Along the way, we all discovered that our two teachers were not only athletic and knowledgeable, but also played instruments. They've really become our heroes; they're wonderful people, and I'm proud to have them as teachers.

Since I take piano lessons, they let me choose a more sophisticated piece: "Amélie's Waltz" by Yann Tiersen. I had just watched *Amélie* (*The Fabulous Destiny of Amélie Poulain*) a few days earlier with Marie and Santi, at Santi's suggestion, actually. The story, the acting, the visual quality of that super poetic film captivated me instantly. I was completely swept away by Tiersen's musical world, carried away like Amélie into daydreams where her imagination wandered... and also as a heroine who takes action to help others despite her shyness! After the first viewing, I already wanted to see it again, or at the very least, replay the soundtrack on rewind. The next day, I asked François to show me the score for "La Valse" so I could learn it as quickly as possible! A real challenge, to be honest—one that just proves how, in the arts, the works that seem the simplest are often the result of a complex process and truly high-level effort. Anyway, the challenge became even tougher when I had to play the piece in class, in front of my friends, at the end of the term. Everyone clapped warmly, so apparently my performance was good enough to impress the students, the teachers, and the few parents who were able to come. Still, I noticed the mistakes, the wrong notes, and the lack of fluidity. Even though I put my whole heart into it, it really wasn't *that* good. But hey, as Santi says, "no self-flagellation—perfection doesn't exist!" I want to do everything perfectly, at school or otherwise, but it really works against me, I know it! And then I procrastinate, turn in my assignments or projects at the last minute. Honestly, I'm just making my own life miserable!

Anyway, to get back to my original topic—what's worrying me the most this week is the final performance for this third term in the arts program. Over the past two and a half months, we've done warm-up and prep exercises for dance and theatre —so far so good—read and analyzed plays, watched classical and contemporary ballet, which was great, but now we actually have to perform or dance in public. I mean, either do a choreography or memorize and speak "loudly and clearly" (thanks, Alex!). For me, that's terrifying. With every session, my anxiety has increased, even though I've tried to follow instructions as best I could. The fatal blow came when Jessica introduced the final project: alone or in a group, we have to create a choreography or choose a play excerpt we like, and stage it! Huge problem for me, who wants to do *neither*: each participant had to speak or dance for two minutes.

Just the thought of this final evaluation sends me into a total panic! And I've known about it since the beginning, yet I've done nothing, literally nothing, to prepare the presentation. I'm paralyzed, as if taking any action would only deepen my dread of the ending. Now we're just a few days away, and I still only have a vague idea of what I could do—knowing full well I probably won't follow through. I tried to bluff my way through with my two teachers, justifying the absence of notes or drafts by saying I'd chosen to dance. "All in my head!" I declared to Jessica, trying to sound confident. I could tell by Jessica's face that she didn't believe it for a second… I bought myself a bit of time, but that doesn't change the fateful date of my performance: my friends and teachers will soon see how poorly I've prepared.

I need to take the "bull by the horns" (another Santi expression) and make the surge of adrenaline that's giving me heart palpitations actually useful! Now it's clear. I can't just do nothing, but I need advice. So, I decide to talk to Santi and Marie. I dash down the stairs two at a time, and burst into the kitchen, only to find myself face-to-face with Marie. In just a few words, I explain the situation and see her face flush red. She looks really angry and starts yelling at me.

"Nana, seriously, why didn't you tell us sooner? Don't you trust us? And now you're backed into a corner! We're not magicians!"

Santi, waiting behind the kitchen island, steps forward and calms things down.

"OK, OK… Nana, I'm sure you understand why we're a little shocked and upset."

He gives Marie a pointed look, and she seems to realize she may have gone too far, before he continues.

"The most important thing is that you finally told us and shared your feelings, your anxiety, instead of keeping it all to yourself. And that's good for you, and encouraging for us. You still trust us, that's clear to me. What about you, Marie?"

"Mmm, yeah, you're right."

"Yes, I'm really sorry. I didn't make the right call. I put off facing it. I shouldn't have…"

Marie answers in a gentler tone now, seeming to have gotten her emotions under control.

"This year, you've dealt with a bunch of challenges in so many areas and you've gotten through most of them successfully. I should have thought about that before snapping at you, and I should've acknowledged it. You've made huge progress, and of course that puts pressure on you. It's normal. We'll always be here for you, you understand?"

"Thank you, really, thank you. I'm truly sorry… but now, I have to do something—it's for the day after tomorrow. What can you suggest? Any ideas?"

Santi is the first to answer.

"My advice? Do something you actually enjoy instead of forcing yourself into something that doesn't appeal to you. It's too late to waste time and energy on an idea that doesn't really excite you. And the result would be even more hit-or-miss."

"Well, choreographing a dance is definitely not for me, even if I like to dance. I enjoy watching theatre, but acting in it, and in front of an audience? No! However, I love writing.

"Yes, but you have to do an oral presentation, Nana!" says Marie, playing the devil's advocate.

Thanks, how is that supposed to help me? My brain is already working at 300%, more intensely than ever: writing *plus* oral presentation, writing *plus* oral presentation… I don't want to dance, and I don't want to recite my text like a robot either. I look up. Santi and Marie are looking at me kindly. He's the one who speaks this time.

"We understand, but why not consider an expressive reading—not acting, but of an original text?"

I look at him blankly.

"Besides your journal, you write poetry, right? Why not some slam poetry?"

Santi's idea is brilliant! In one second, I'm convinced it's the right one, the solution to my problem. Whenever I'm overwhelmed by emotions, no matter what causes them, I turn them into poems.

"It's true, I love writing and poetry, and I can present in front of the class, especially if I'm reading one of my own pieces, no problem. Thank you, Marie, thank you, Santi, you're lifesavers. I'm going to try, but I need to get Jessica and Alex's permission first."

"Send them a message right now! he urges with enthusiasm. If they agree, you start tonight, right after dinner. We can even talk about the theme or your perspective while we eat, if you want to. It's totally up your alley!"

He seems even more excited about the idea than I am, even though *he's* not the one who has to write a whole poem in one evening! I send the message immediately. The reply arrives less than five minutes later, probably the time it took Alex and Jessica to consult each other. And it's a yes! With one condition: since I'm presenting my own text and I'm allowed to read it (thank you, slam rules!), I'll have to do it in public, during one of the monthly poetry nights organized at school. Even though I've never been to one, obviously, I've heard of them. They call them *Poetry on Stage*. The two teachers are making me pay the price for not following the original instructions! Jessica's message explains their decision. She speaks about fairness toward the other students who will present a choreography or a theatre piece tomorrow and the day after. I understand.

But that name says it all: *on stage*, not just in front of the class or a few parents! Suddenly, the anxiety rushes back in, my heart is pounding. Should I drop the idea and scramble to find another? No, it's too late! Could I conveniently fall ill on the evening of performance, three days from now? No. First, that wouldn't be right. I'm tired of backing out and running away. And it wouldn't be cool for anyone, not for Santi and Marie, nor for Alex and Jessica, after all the support they've given me, and Jessica's accommodation. I'll move forward with it, full steam ahead!

Four hours later, I emerge from my trance-like state, and look up at my phone. It's 1:00 a.m., a little late, but not too late if I can calm my excitement and catch a few hours of sleep. The text is there, in front of me—three pages of poetry that I'll be slamming on Saturday. Sure, there'll be a few tweaks, some language editing, maybe a final review by Marie or Santi if they're around. I'm quite proud of myself.

No one warned me! I could've been curious and asked in advance. The evening seemed like it would go well. I was focused, ready to face down a handful of "tortured poets" and introverts, lovers of obscure verses and flat rhymes. Instead, hidden behind a curtain, I'm looking at a packed student café. It's full of young people, and not just from my school. There are a lot of new faces out there. The noise is overwhelming and kind of dizzying, but I have to admit, there's a positive vibe coming off the crowd, all gathered around round bistro tables. The lighting in the room is dim, except for the spotlight on the stage, where I'm standing. Right in the middle, there's a mic on a stand just waiting for me (and the other performers) to bring it to life and let it do its thing.

I'm so nervous my legs feel like jelly, I'm weak and my hands are all clammy. You can still make out people's faces, and I spot Santi and Marie sitting at a table off to the side, not front row, thankfully. Oh! Alex just walked in, then Jessica. They join my parents!

The hosts tonight are a teacher I've seen in the hallways. She teaches French, I think, and she's the one who started the school's slam club, and a senior who seems to pop up at every event as an emcee. He's super chill when speaking in public and always throws in jokes during his intros. Just knowing he'll warm up the crowd before I go up makes me feel a tiny bit better.

I won't be going on first. So, I was told yesterday. But now I learn that I'll be performing *last* because they had to add me at the last minute, and it was too late to change the printed posters and flyers. On social media and the school website, my name is there, though. Aïcha pointed it out the moment it was posted, and made sure to spread the word! Despite me ghosting her party at the beginning of the year and refusing to join the basketball team, she didn't hold a grudge. That's just how she is. She sulked for a few days, then let it go. In fact, she promised to come with the whole basketball team tonight, and they're all here now, at a table to the right. Besides the fact that some of them are really tall, they're so loud you can't miss them. But it still warms my heart. I have to rise to the occasion. I try to focus.

The next hour passes in a blur, as I alternate between sitting and pacing away from the stage… and away from prying eyes. I hear the others perform, one after the other, as if I were behind a thick curtain, not even noticing the people moving around me. Until a hand grabs my arm and yanks me out of my trance.

"Nana, it's your turn! Yoo-hoo, can you hear me? Dimitri just wrapped up, and you need to go on stage!"

It's a rude awakening. I see myself walking toward the curtain as the host announces me as the final performer of the evening and gives the title of my poem. Out of the corner of my eye, through the curtains, a splash of orange in the front row catches my attention. I stop for a second, locking eyes with an intense gaze. It's Lucie! She came too—without telling me —but it doesn't matter! I could panic, but I don't. A warm feeling spreads through me, I even manage a little smile. I look at my hands. They're trembling slightly, but holding my text firmly, not tensely. My heart is racing, but I feel focused, suddenly calmer.

The music I chose starts—*Oliassa*. It's time to step into the spotlight, facing the indistinct crowd now gone silent. I stand before the mic and open my mouth to whisper a timid good evening, before lowering my eyes to the sheet in front of me.

Cinderella Risen from the Deep

Like a tale from some old book,

But here—every word is true,

And every word is made up too.

So open your minds,

Sharpen your appetite.

You'll get a dose of little lies,

And big truths that bite,

No matter your age,

Your sex, your body, your name, your fight.

I'm a girl made of porcelain.

They? Elephants.

Crashing through my space,

Dragging me into playground games,

Where someone always gets bruised,

Where the crowd moves smooth,

And erases whoever doesn't fit the groove.

Too often, we walk

Among fragile things—

Our neighbours, our lovers, our kin—

And smash them,

With hands too rough,

Words too blunt,

Hearts too shut.

So I move slow—

Step by step,

Sketching my own path,

Skipping the ruts and the wreckage,

Crossing this life,

Light-footed,

Sinking my teeth into it,

Without ever losing my bite.

My ears ring,

My voice hums,

My skin still echoes,

The thousand faces,

The thousand threats,

I've crossed and survived.

I'm in the dark,

But my eyes stay open.

I doubt,

But my head stays high.

My trembling body waits—

Still, silent—

For the first little boat,

To come passing by.

Just a nutshell, maybe,

To lift me up and tell Death,

Not today.

Not today, Grim Sister—

You won't have me,
Not this fragile thing,
Still crying for help.

And I start to dream,
In black and white,
Of childhood moments,
Buried deep in the sands of memory—
An endless sun,
Dunes on every side,
The scent of sour milk,
And smoke from spiced pots.
I hear the goats of Mauritania—
Their bleating, a holy song.
I see them leaping,
Dancing with the wind,
As if they too,
Are trying to forget.

And I dream of that dry land—
My town, my wrinkled grandparents,
Whom I left,
Without turning back.
Nothing but my feet,
To carry me across the waves,

Just a breath, a hope,
To rewrite my fate.

Dreams are windows—
Wide open to greener grass,
To a world not yet broken.
They pull us toward the Beautiful,
Inspire us to press on,
To hold tight,
To never give in.
And believe me—
In the name of my people,
And the freedom that waits,
Around the corner—
Dreams are real.
Not science, maybe,
But I know it deep.
As real as you,
As real as this stage,
As real as the glass in your hand.

Now, about freedom—
Mine doesn't come cheap.
Or rather, it costs everything.
The price?
My whole life, over and again.

I had to leave mine behind,
Drag myself along a thorny road
I barely believed in.
Never again, I said—
Better to walk away,
Leave behind the path of martyrs.
Abandon friends, family, my country.
Get lost a hundred times,
In the hands of monsters,
With no god and no law—
All to finally find my way,
To find my voice,
And lift it up.

And if some speak with fists,
With vocal cords frayed raw,
For me, all it takes is,
A pen and paper.
Anywhere, anytime.
Writing is sacred—
It's the magic wand,
That turns dreams to facts
And balances this brutal world,
With ink.

Not long ago,

My heart hit pause—

Halftime in a game I didn't ask to play.

Something deep inside said:

"Rest. Obey. Survive."

It curled up black,

Bruised and bloodied,

By too many hits,

Too many stories,

Too many bodies frozen in grief.

That mighty, broken muscle,

Just wanted out—

To break through my ribs,

And burst into the sky.

But now—

Now my life is repopulated.

It teems with kindness,

With warmth,

With hands that reached into my cave,

And pulled me back into light.

My inner world has shape again,

Relief, colour, form.

And sure, I still drift—

Still hide in the cool shade,

Of a secret desert pool.

Still let my thoughts swim,

Through the holes in my memory.

But I know now:

That pain wasn't wasted.

Those wounds made my armour.

And now—finally—

I can break my chains.

And among all the living pillars,

Of this temple I carry inside—

There is one,

More than just an ally.

She keeps my heart beating.

I never tell her enough—

I want to bury her in kisses.

"Here, take my flowers, my fruit,

My branches, my blood."

Not Verlaine—I fumble my lines.

But instead of "you," I'd just say "us."

Forgive me if, from]here on,

I speak to just one soul—

The one who crossed paths,

With my fatal path,

One night,

Over a ball—
Lucie.

You showed me a road,
So bright, so wide,
That it could hold two futures.
You are my sister-in-arms,
On the rugby field,
But more than that,
You're the soul-sister,
Who always wipes my tears.

Now—
Lean in, listen close...
I won't end this with more words,
But with music.

Because music is everything:
Words are music,
Eyes are music,
Touch is music.
And everything around us—
This whole world—
Is just an invitation,
To join the song.

Maybe music won't save the world—
But it saved me,
One day on the Mediterranean,
Not so long ago.

We're all born as blank sheets,
But life dresses us in notes.
And we search—
For harmony,
For a heart that'll play alongside ours.

We cross oceans and continents,
From the country within us,
In search of better days.
We are perfect instruments,
In a score written just for us—
From moderato to allegro,
Faster and faster,
Through painful scherzos,
To a final fortissimo,
That earns us, at last,
A little rest.

Thank you.

TOULOUSE, FRIDAY, MAY 24, 2024

Another week comes to an end, adding to the feeling of closure, of inevitable finality. It's not just in the air—it's real. As real as the applause that filled the student café last Saturday, echoing the words I had just spoken moments earlier. Carried by my verses, I had spent those two minutes fiercely struggling to lift my head from the pages and face the audience. When I finally bowed to the crowd, I caught Adam—Karen's boyfriend —staring at me with an unreadable smile: was it under-standing? Admiration? Mockery? I left the stage happy, but with a strange knot in my stomach. Lucie joined me behind the curtains, now drawn, and quickly made me forget that odd feeling.

In any case, things are moving fast, and today is the deadline for handing in our year-end projects—an important milestone in the school year, especially for us in the integration class. This year, we entered a new school system, and for most of us, a new country as well. It's the perfect opportunity to show who we are, in a format that fits us. I'm just repeating what Jessica said when she introduced the project. Basically, I chose a topic, did some research around a central question, and then put together a written report over the weeks—mostly during class—about ten pages long. I'll present it orally in June to a "jury" (Marc, Jessica, and the assistant principal). Now that many memories of my life before the shipwreck have come back and with all the work done with the psychologist, the topic was almost obvious: *"Living in the Mauritanian desert: a sustainable option?"* That's the subject I chose, and through this project, I was able to showcase what I've learned in geography, biology and health, even history—and of course, French. Marc and Jessica congratulated me this week on the quality of my French, and also on the improvement in my grades. With a bit of extra help after school, I've taken back control of my studies, and my marks have already started to go up. With one exception: math. That's still not going so well, and they advised me to head more towards literature and languages next year, in *Première*. I'll still have math, but at a less advanced level, which suits me just fine! Anyway, I'm proud to have finished on time: my appendectomy is just a memory now, and I can focus on studying for our final exams. All of this has kept my mind busy, but in a good way. I had all the time I needed to polish those projects, which really count toward our average.

Without any physical activity since the infamous operation, I've felt truly rested. I was playing the piano not just once but twice a day, with growing joy. And I had time to reflect on a lot of things. That first week, bedridden, I had a moment of despair, wondering if my teammates had forgotten me, if I still had a place on the team—on any team—after my recovery. Had my physical condition deteriorated too much in the meantime? I received a few messages of encouragement on social media, but fewer than I expected. I was genuinely worried.

Then, in the second week, I had visitors, first my rugby sevens team, accompanied by Emma. Almost all the girls came to my house, bringing a beautiful bouquet of flowers and candy. While the coach stayed downstairs chatting with my parents, we hung out in my room. I could get up and walk— with the soft melodies of Hamzo Bryn in the background. And we stuffed ourselves with candy, so amazing! We caught up on all the latest gossip, talked about the training sessions, and even the "damn tournament." On that front, they seemed to have kinda come to terms with the losses—partly thanks to Claire, who had dropped by to watch one of their practices. Our scrum-half was planning to get back into training by the end of the month, and maybe even play in the last tournament in June, as long as she followed the return-to-play protocol. The whole team seemed to be *r-r-ragaillardi*, pumped up (to really appreciate the word you have to say its "r" with a deep Southwestern French accent!). As for me, I felt relieved and genuinely excited to get back on the rugby field. I seriously couldn't wait!

After the girls left, to my surprise, Emma asked if I had a few minutes to talk.

"Nana, you seem to be doing well."

"Yes, I'm feeling great. When can I start training again?"

"That's for your doctor to decide. You're lucky to have one at home. That might speed things up. Your parents, Marc, and I are going to prepare a gradual return-to-play plan so that you'll be able to participate in both the final rugby sevens tournament and one or both of the last fifteen-a-side games. Just like I promised."

My chest almost burst with happiness. Everything could go back to the way it was! I was speechless and couldn't hold back a few tears. She gave my shoulder a gentle pat and continued.

"That's normal. It's okay. Focus on school. We'll handle the rest. First, your parents will bring you to training so you can observe and ease back in. It's good to watch from the outside once in a while. Then you'll resume jogging—I think you've got your routine. After that, some light speed training, with Marc supervising it. After all that, you'll return to non-contact practice, including some kicking. Sound good?"

"Yes, coach. Thank you so much, I don't know how to…"

Ah! I kept crying, but this time she hugged me tightly without saying a word, waved goodbye to my parents, and left.

The second visit, this afternoon, completely lit up my week. Saying it was just a ray of sunshine would be a gross understatement and a bit of a cliché. It was more like a full sunbath, the kind that nourishes both your body and soul for a good while. As usual, Santi and Marie were off doing their late-afternoon sports. I was alone, in pajamas, a book on my lap in bed, hadn't even washed all day! I heard the doorbell. Who could it be? I opened the door cautiously… Lucie? I hadn't seen her in what felt like forever. She was wearing a short light green skirt that showed off her toned, tanned legs and a tight white top that gaped slightly between her breasts. How could I look away from that invitation and meet her eyes? Her ponytail framed her freckled, babyish face. Now my eyes were fixed on her lips, so close I could smell their tangy scent, blending with the fragrance of her skin. She looks good enough to eat… and me, I look like a total wreck. I give her a half-hearted, awkward smile.

"Well, this is a surprise…"

Those were the only words I could manage.

"Hey, am I interrupting? Good surprise or bad?"

We'd been texting since my operation, but I was afraid that distance had become an obstacle. Deep down, I secretly hoped she'd make the first move. Instead of answering, I swallowed hard. I wanted so badly to kiss her, to press myself against her, and then, maybe if… But seeing her in person threw me off. A wave of heat rose to my cheeks. I kissed her awkwardly and took her hand, leading her to the living room. Then I rushed to the bathroom upstairs without saying a word.

"Nana, what are you doing? Are you okay? Should I come back another day?"

"No, no, definitely not! I'm just changing. I'll be right with you."

Those were the last words we exchanged. A few minutes later, as I returned to my bedroom after showering, the towel still wrapped around my chest, I froze. Lucie was there. She was walking around my room. I watched in silence. She hadn't heard me come in. She ran her fingers over the sheets on my bed, stopped at one of my photos, held my pajamas to her face. When she sees me, she doesn't seem surprised and walks straight toward me. No words needed! We kiss, and I dare to slip my tongue into her mouth. Effortlessly, she pushes me down onto the bed. I flip her over, she flips me back. My towel vanishes as if by magic. Lucie surprises me with new caresses; our embraces feel both familiar and fresh. I pull down her zipper, and her skirt falls to the floor around us. From her thighs, I discover the exquisite paleness of her skin up to the faint line where her shorts once were. In one swift motion, she takes off her t-shirt—her round breasts with wide areolas bloom before my eyes. Pressed tightly together, seismic tremors shake our bellies, only to melt into unspoken heat. A whisper, then silence between breaths, while her tongue still plays over my skin and between my thighs. It's so intense, I want to dive deeper, immerse myself entirely. But she rises, takes my face in her open palms, her gaze engulfs me. I'm even more aroused. She kisses me slowly... Our hands drift downward, slower this time, toward each other's sex. We allow ourselves to climax loudly, as if nothing and no one else existed. Each of her cries is echoed by one of my moans. Lucie releases a wave of heat inside me, which my organism embraces.

And then, we let ourselves drift peacefully into the drowsiness that follows love. One last caress to the damp folds of our bodies, the sun sets over us, a serene joy grips me. I also rest just for a moment.

"Honey, we're back! Everything okay?

I spring from the bed as if stung by a scorpion! How long have I been asleep? What time is it? Where am I? For a second, I think I'm in my room with its ochre clay walls in Chinguetti! Marie's soprano voice has yanked me out of a heavy, dreamless sleep. Beside me, Lucie is also waking, startled, as if caught in the act. She jumps out of bed and scrambles to get dressed. But suddenly, I realize something in me has changed. Why don't I feel guilt or anxiety?

I turn to Lucie.

"Take your time, no worries. We'll go down together anyway. Don't be embarrassed. Let me handle this?"

Without waiting for her reply, I kiss her and call out to Marie:

"Yes, everything's fine, Marie. I'm with Lucie. We'll be down in a minute."

A few minutes later, we are *débarbouillées*, freshened up (what a delightfully sensual word!), and head toward the stairs. There's a fairly long hallway to cross. As we reach the first step, I slip my hand into Lucie's without warning and squeeze it tight. She doesn't pull away—instead, she grips mine back.

And that's how we go to meet my parents! They'd stopped at the corner store to pick up a few last-minute groceries and are already in the kitchen unpacking the bags. Bobette comes bounding toward us, barking happily. Marie looks us over as if nothing is out of the ordinary, handing us each an apple. Santi turns around, and I see his eyes pause for the briefest second on our clasped hands before looking up at me. I ask, in the most innocent tone:

"Can Lucie stay for dinner tonight?"

"When there's enough for three, there's enough for four, right?"

TOULOUSE, SUNDAY, JUNE 9, 2024

At dawn, for no particular reason, I woke up spontaneously. I turned on my clock radio... "Completely crazy"? That set the tone for the day! I couldn't go back to sleep anyway. Thoughts and images were spinning around in my head—I may have absorbed a bit too much of Emma's mental visualization technique. Now it was time to take action, so I turned on my phone and found a good stretch-strengthening video. I did my first stretches in just underwear and a tank top, bouncing in rhythm until the floor shook, then dropped to the ground to finish the session. I checked every muscle, every joint, including my fingers, hips, and abs. All my injuries and scars went through a thorough examination; I didn't want to leave anything to chance. And miracle of miracles—so to speak, given the effort in physiotherapy, exercise, and patience it had taken—no post-exercise pain!

Marie finally came bounding up the stairs, three at a time, to see if everything was okay. She came in without knocking, looking worried, and before she could utter a single word, I stopped her.

"Everything's fine. I couldn't sleep anymore. So I did a little session to see how my body would react. All good, I'm ready to play in the tournament!"

I stood up and jogged in place like a boxer, miming uppercuts and punches. Marie smiled again and stepped toward me.

"Okay, fine, you've convinced me. We'll take you to the meeting point in forty-five minutes. This time, the ride to the tournament is only an hour. You'll get there early enough."

"Good, I'll meet you downstairs for breakfast."

Barely two hours later, we were walking toward the locker rooms. It was already the third and final tournament of our season! I was thrilled to finally pick up where I had left off several weeks earlier. During our last practices, I'd actually surprised myself—my reflexes seemed to have come back on their own (passes, runs, shots, combinations). Today, my mind was telling me that this was a critical moment for the team, but my heart and body felt simply happy and at peace. I just wanted to experience the pure joy of playing my favourite sport, of being with my teammates and coach, here and now.

Santi and Marie dropped me off at the main Argoulets parking lot, and I headed straight for the locker room, where nearly all the girls were already gathered. The music was blasting, as usual. As soon as I walked in, I had to cóver my ears—I was met with shrieks of welcome, and soon I was buried under hugs. No one had really expected me to be there!

Once the greetings were over, I quietly went through my ritual: shorts, jersey, socks, cleats; two wraps of laces around each shoe; a double knot for each. Then, mouthguard check, hair inspection, and double-check that my jersey was tucked into my shorts. Nothing was sticking out—I was ready.

The warm-up felt like a dream. I feel every part of my feet engaging as I launch into my sprints. In the second phase of my stride, my torso opens up, driven by the rhythmic swing of my arms, channelling all my power forward. I'm confident, though I can't explain why—clear-headed, alert. Our opponents have never looked more ready to bring us down. Most of them have done it before. But that gives us the edge. Their overconfidence might make them let down their guard.

We played the *Molosses* first. True to form, they relied on their size and weight to hurt us in contact. We'd planned to punish them properly after what they did to us in the last tournament. "Break out the spiked helmets!" Emma had said. This time, we held our ground by consistently going low on front tackles and grabbing their ankles. My turn came in the second half, playing as a winger. I even stopped them from scoring a try with a beautiful tackle from behind, followed by a fast ruck rugby sevens style, since I managed to get back on my feet immediately. A minute or two later, their centre—built like a tank—charged at me at full speed. I realized she meant to run right over me. Instead of stopping, I kept running, slowing gradually, then at the last second, I dropped to one knee and pushed hard with my thighs at the point of contact, and took her down! It was still a defensive tackle—one that absorbed her momentum—but she lost the ball on impact. Like before, I popped back up, grabbed the ball, and sprinted eighty metres to score under the posts.

On top of that, I made all the conversions, adding two points to each try. At the final whistle, we were ahead by four points.

"Ladies, there's no such thing as a small win. So, congratulations! Stretching routine, hydration, you can eat a bit, but not too much, and eat something that digests fast. We'll meet back here in thirty minutes."

The next two games proved that our humility and hard work at training had helped each of us level up and develop our potential. We played our best rugby of the season against opponents who had taken their win for granted. In the first case, they hadn't found any reliable kickers to take kickoffs, penalties, or conversions—all drop kicks in rugby sevens. That made the difference. On our team, three of us shared the work:

kickoffs, long kicks toward the posts, short sideline kicks. We made every single kick, racking up as many points as possible.

In the other game, the final one, things were much closer. Their team played a style similar to ours, with roughly the same strengths and weaknesses. However, individually, we had the edge. Claire had only played the second half of the second game, but Emma put her in from the start this time. Finally back in the game, she had so much energy and enthusiasm that she unleashed a flurry of moves: quick inside passes out of the breakdown, up-and-under kicks, dummy passes followed by breaks through the defence from a ruck. She even scored two tries by taking quick penalty taps, not giving our stunned opponents time to retreat the required ten metres. I added a low kick that allowed Laura—also returning from a concussion—to score a try!

A kind of euphoria swept over us as the second half wore on. "The tables have turned," said Emma laconically after the game.

As the afternoon drew to a close, tired but happy, we gathered in a circle one last time before the final game of the day. We were actually about to play an unofficial season final. Thanks to our wins, we had climbed back to second place, and one more victory would put us ahead by a single point. As luck would have it, we were up against the girls from Perpignan, who had beaten us twice hands down. Emma gave her coach's talk, Claire, our captain, spoke too, but this time I decided to share my feelings with the group. It couldn't hurt, as my therapist would say. I raised my hand to ask if I could speak, and Emma nodded.

"We're killing it, girls! I'm so proud of you! Can you believe we were practically newbies at sevens not that long ago? Okay, fine—me even more than you! But just look at how far we've come. The highs, the lows, the great plays and the screw-ups—the ones we took… and the ones we dished out. And here we are again, all of us together, doing what we love most: playing rugby! I'm seriously proud to be here with you. And there's nowhere else I'd rather be today. Out there, I won't back down. I won't let them walk all over me. I don't know about you, but I'm going all in for this final game of the season. And no matter what happens, my heart stays with rugby sevens. Promise. You with me?

"Yes!"

"We're not letting them walk all over us this time, right?"

"No!"

"Okay!"

They all reply in unison. We're fired up as we shout our team cheer just before getting into position on the field. Emma puts me in from the first half, and I feel slightly intoxicated—the noise, the smell of sweat that comes before the effort, the scent of freshly cut grass—it all goes to my head. Spectators from all over stayed for what promised to be the highlight of the day, and the stands were packed. The players from the fifteen-a-side team had come to support us—they who had dominated their pool all season long. Their banners and cheers stood out clearly.

We're the "receiving" team, so the opposition will kick off —the referee's coin toss decided it. The tension is palpable. I squint; the sun is low and blinding. I should expect a high kick. I've taken time to circle the field again, to take in its dimensions, spot irregularities in the turf, and feel it out almost like an animal. I saw a documentary about players, especially kickers, who get to know their turf this way. It's also a great way to enter the game fully focused. Finally, after the referee asks each captain if their team is ready, he blows the whistle and the ball soars high toward our twenty-two-meter line. It's coming straight at me.

The rest isn't the epic battle we were hoping for, but a game where we defend our honour with heart. We're playing just as well as we did in our previous games. The hitch is that our opponents really know their rugby. They dominate the breakdowns, reposition themselves quickly and flawlessly, and their passes are sharp and powerful. They play a lot, and play well, through the deep middle, charging into every opening without hesitation, throwing our defence off balance. At the rucks, they recycle the ball at a dizzying pace—so fast, in fact, that by the time we get there to make the tackle, they've already moved it on. It feels like they're always one step ahead, and we end up offside more than once.

Thankfully, we hold onto the ball, pass it cleanly, and seize every chance to score, even if those chances are few. At halftime, we're twelve points behind: two tries, one converted. The brief break changes nothing—if anything, it makes things worse. We stop scoring tries early in the second half, and despite pushing up on defence, our tackles aren't enough. No matter how hard we try, the game is slipping away. We pour our last drops of energy into these final minutes. All the substitutes have come in over the course of the game and done their part, but you can feel a deep fatigue that our enthusiasm can no longer overcome. Finally, our persistent defensive pressure causes a knock-on from our opponents. One last scrum is called in our forty-metre zone, roughly mid-field. Laura and I run to speak to Claire.

"Claire, wait! Want to try something? We've got nothing to lose, right? Call for the "69"!"

"But we've never done it in a game!"

"Well, there's a first time for everything. Think of it as our last stand. And anyway, most of it's on you. No pressure, right?"

"Not sure, but okay."

The "69" (yes, I know, but we can have a laugh sometimes, can't we?) is a play that includes a kind of reversal. The trick is to misdirect the opposing team's attention to allow for a kick and a run down the opposite wing, with a final inside pass. In my opinion (and Marie's), it's one of the most beautiful things movement-based rugby has to offer. The referee quickly calls us back to get the scrum going—the ball will be out fast.

"Crouch! Bind! Set!"

Claire feeds the ball into the scrum and immediately recovers it from the feet of the hooker. Meanwhile, the backline, the number 5, and Laura, playing 6, break away from the left side of the attack line and sprint to the right of the scrum to call for the ball. The entire opposing defence shifts in sync to block what looks like an attack forming on that side. The scrum-half fakes a pass to the right, just like in a standard play. I'm the only one who stayed on the left—I'm gauging the distance I need to cover and how fast I'll need to go in the first phase, determined to give it my all in the second to carry the ball as far as I can. I close my eyes for a second, visualize the trajectory, feel my weight shift onto my left leg, take a deep breath, and I take off. Claire, instead of passing right, surprises them by kicking high and long over the defence toward the left, risking a touch-line kick. My run is diagonal, and I push even harder to stay perfectly timed to catch the ball. I reach up and grab it just before it goes out.

From there, the goal: the try line. I sprint like a rocket. The crowd noise explodes—it's wild in the stands! I know the opposing winger is not only experienced, but faster than the fastest—definitely faster than me. She's scored enough tries and shut down enough of our attacks to be unforgettable.

But the "69" has another surprise in store. It includes a second movement: just as the kick went up, with all eyes on the ball and the landing zone, Laura began crossing the field toward me, straight toward the corner where I was headed. At the very moment I'm tackled from behind, I'm about ten metres from the try line. Just as planned, I know Laura is on my right. I offload the ball blind, right after contact. And as expected, no one else followed, and she touches it down between the posts. The whole team rushes over, as if we'd won. The conversion is a formality, but we still lose the game. We all gave 100% out there, and strangely, even though the scoreboard says otherwise, it feels like a real win. Our fans go wild—they storm the field at the final whistle to lift us up. We ended up finishing second in the regional championship after this tournament, and we have no regrets.

The third half was incredible. First, a memorable party at a restaurant that went late into the night, with players from both teams in attendance. Even Karen, the hooker from the fifteen-a-side team, was there with her brooding, artfully dishevelled boyfriend. From her seat, she gave me a thumbs-up and a big, seemingly genuine smile. Had her feelings toward me changed? I dared to believe so. Still, I'd given up trying to figure out that guy and their relationship—they hadn't shown a shred of friendliness at school all year! Parents, volunteers, club members, and even the men's teams were invited. Between courses, we danced. I had personally invited Marc and

Jessica. Lucie had gone her own way after the game but rejoined me at the start of the dinner. Emma gently reminded me at the start of the evening that I had a final game coming up with the fifteen-a-side team the next Saturday, and then I didn't see her again until Tuesday's practice. I promised her I'd be careful and present at both prep sessions. I was flattered—honoured—to be able to play that final game with the A team. Six months earlier, that had been all I could dream of. But that didn't change anything—I had made my decision: next year, I would not only continue playing rugby sevens, but I was even planning to try out for the regional team. And maybe more, if things went well.

For now, though, the mood was all about celebration. The place was packed—we had filled the restaurant in no time flat. Even the terrace was full. It felt a bit like the beginning of the end for us young people, as our year-end exam period was just days away.

At the end of the meal, and as usual, Alex issued an invitation. The message popped up instantly on everyone's phone. The after-party was now happening at her place. Only for the club's players and their friends. That still made quite a crowd. After asking my parents' permission and promising them that Lucie would drive me back, we left the adults and headed out to her car.

The thirty-minute drive took an hour, because we wanted to celebrate the win in our own way, just the two of us. She pulled over into a parking area just past one of the many bends that dotted the hillside road above the city. After a moment of silence, Lucie turned to me. She restarted the conversation with meaningless small talk. We both knew it was just chatter, but I played along. I replied, nodded, agreed. And I looked at her. Or rather, I stared at her. She had let down her hair, which now fell over her shoulders and gave off a captivating fragrance. I took a deep breath. I was savouring the moment. She understood. But she kept talking as if nothing was happening. Still, I saw her nostrils flaring just a little faster. The temperature in the car was gradually rising. Then my gaze moved to her lips, to her cheeks that had begun to blush, to her little round-tipped nose. The adrenaline from the win was still coursing through my veins. I felt a wave of desire spread to the tips of my limbs. At the slightest movement I made, I could see her pupils shift quickly. I felt an inexplicable joy and an unshakable confidence. A moment later, our noses brushed. Then, suddenly, intensely, we rediscovered the sweetness of our mouths. My cheeks were burning. I stroked her in rhythm while she clung to me. Then she flipped me over. We whispered magical, unheard-of words to each other. "Your breasts charm me with their warmth"; "You are the spring that quenches and satisfies me"; "You are the full moon that lights my way"; "You hold the thread of my life in your hands"; "You are my muse, my sister, my lover."

I was in bliss. Not long after, beaming, we rejoined our teammates with enthusiasm. The party was already in full swing, despite the late hour. As always, the alcohol was flowing and the music was drawing a crowd, both inside and outside the house. This time, the revellers had even spilled into the park out front of the kind of mansion where Alex lived. You could make out their silhouettes quite clearly, as the full moon bathed the scene in a spectral light. We toasted to our victory several times—basically, every time we ran into another group of players. I even had to celebrate this memorable day with Karen, who offered me a drink! How could I refuse? The enthusiasm and generosity of my teammates were so contagious!

After the drinks, joints began to circulate. We danced like mad without paying much attention to the time. Around two in the morning, I started to get tired. My legs felt heavy. Was it the combination of muscle fatigue, the bit of alcohol I'd had, and whatever I'd smoked? I felt dizzy... a little woozy. My blood throbbed at my temples. I apologized to Lucie and headed toward the living room. Rather than walk around the house, I wanted to cut through it to rest in the park out front, where the air would be fresher and the music much quieter. Lucie walked off to grab something to drink; she still felt like dancing and had the energy for it. So I let her go her way, certain we'd find each other later.

When I got there, I sat on one of the low sculptures that flanked the path to the house. My thoughts were jumbled, my legs weak—I would've gladly lain down for a few minutes in the moonlight.

Suddenly, I had the feeling of being watched. I turned around: Karen's boyfriend was walking slowly in my direction. But I didn't see her, which surprised me, since they were usually inseparable. Then again, I wasn't with my better half either. So I stayed put. He walked toward me, eyes fixed on mine, as if trying to hypnotize me, but without the hostility that had characterized our previous encounters. I met his gaze squarely, trying to smile, despite the growing urge to close my eyes.

"Hi, Fatimata."

"Hey, Noah, how are you?"

"Yeah, not bad. I have to say, you really impressed me this afternoon. You were glowing out there."

"Thanks. What's with all the compliments?"

"And you're even more beautiful tonight! Honest truth. I've wanted to tell you for a while. I like you, a lot. Not very original, I know, but there it is. There's this little spark about you, an indefinable charm, that makes you so beautiful!"

He delivered his monologue like a love-struck teen making his first declaration. It was kind of sweet. My eyelids were heavy. Now he was avoiding my gaze. He seemed embarrassed, which showed a different, more vulnerable side of him. It was touching, even though there was zero chance anything would ever happen between us. Did he seriously believe what he was saying?

"Wow, I'm surprised. I didn't see that coming. Is this a confession of love?"

My question went unanswered. But then Noah suddenly lunged toward me! In the same motion, he grabbed me from behind and clamped his hand over my mouth. For a moment, I panicked, but a surge of adrenaline kicked in. He brought his mouth close to my neck; I could hear and feel his booze-laced breath in my left ear. He sniffed my skin and murmured:

"You know what? I've been into you from the start, from the first time I saw you. I really want to get to know you better. You're going to say, 'I have a girlfriend,' but deep down, I think you prefer men. Going for girls—that's a mistake. It's not natural. You're just confused, a little lost, it's normal. Tonight, I'm going to show you how good it can feel with a man. You'll come back to the right side, you'll see… You're going to love it!"

I understood all too well what that meant—no way I was going through that again! I tried to scream "No! No!" but couldn't, as he held my head so tight. I struggled to free my mouth. Impossible! I could only try to scream through his hand, or bite anything I could. The second my teeth sank into his dangling index finger, he howled. He jumped back, clutching his hand and swearing. I sprang up and kicked him hard in the groin. First, he doubled over, then collapsed, writhing on the ground in louder cries of pain than before.

I managed to move forward, even began to run. I reached the trees of the park. I saw Lucie coming out the front door just as my legs gave out. I collapsed to my knees on the gravel. I felt no pain, just a kind of heavy languor, and my vision blurred... An overwhelming fatigue washed over me... Strangely, I watched myself close my eyes, thinking: *just for a few seconds...*

She looks at her reflection in the water of the bucket at her feet. She's five years old. Long, thick, dirty hair. It'll need to be washed tonight. Oiled. And combed at length. She likes the feeling of the comb on the top of her scalp. You can pull her hair—it doesn't bother her. She studies her rather delicate features for a Haratine. Big, doe-like eyes. Maybe it's the first time she's become aware of her body. Behind her, she hears laughter. She turns around. Her big brother is mocking her with his friends.

"So, Nana, aren't you tired of admiring your reflection? You think you'll turn into a flower? Then we'll just pick you..."

She doesn't understand the innuendo. But the tone—yes. Mocking and vaguely threatening. She's afraid. She looks left, right. No one. Just abandoned streets in the middle of the desert.

"Hey, guys, let's help her out! What if we *planted* her like a flower. Such a pretty flower!"

As he says this, he steps closer. She is paralyzed by fear. He grabs her arm.

"Ow! That hurts! Let me go, Maatallah!"

Another hand, not her brother's, touches her, probes her. She feels it through her t-shirt.

"I'm going to tell Daddy!"

"Come on, little sister… We're going to plant you in the ground like a beautiful flower ready to be picked! You'll love it…"

"To the *guelta*!"

She's lifted and carried like a piece of cargo. Over Youssouf's shoulder. Her brother's best friend. And the tallest of the gang. They quickly reach the edge of the village. The dunes are there. The *guelta* not far now. She sees the waterhole and the palm trees too. She's been there before, but always with her mother.

The boys are taking this very seriously. Two of them hold her. They grip her arms and cover her mouth. She gives up struggling quickly. They're too strong, these big boys. And what's the point of screaming? It's too hot. Everyone's inside at this time of day. No one will hear. No one will come.

The other three find the spot where the digging is easiest. They do it with their hands. Since she's small, no need to go deep.

"Come on, in the hole, pretty flower!"

But—but—no! She can't believe it. They're really going to do it.

"Naked now! In Eve's clothing! That'll be your punishment, woman!"

She doesn't understand much. But she feels the boys' hands lift her t-shirt. Undo the button on her shorts. Their hands on her body. They pull off her socks and her underwear. Naked in front of the boys. She clumsily places her hand over her sex. Like she was taught to do. Her brother lifts her and plants her in the hole. She can barely move. Only her head sticks out.

Why? Why?

The five boys get to work. They refill the hole. It doesn't take long. She can't move at all now.

"We'll come get you after the siesta, okay?"

They turn their backs. Run away.

"Hey! Hey! Come back!"

No one. Just the scorching sun. She sweats heavily. Her mouth goes dry. After a while, her head begins to hurt. She so badly wants to close her eyes. Just rest for a few seconds. From time to time, she opens her eyes. Not for long. But enough to observe. To see the life of the desert from ground level. It's new and strange.

Her attention is caught by movement around her. Even in the height of the heat, the desert is alive! She's never noticed this before. She's astonished. The nearby spring draws wildlife.

Slender-horned oryx, snow-white addax, fennec foxes with huge ears, desert partridges, shrews, lizards of all sizes. She herself is slowly roasting. She catches glimpses of insects usually too small to see.

Night soon falls. Blessed relief. And the moon rises. Full, whole, majestic.

Suddenly, a scorpion approaches, lit by the spectral moonlight. It's as black as the moon, small, and moves quickly. She knows these are the worst. It seems to know where it's going. Toward her!

She closes her eyes. She's dreaming. I'm dreaming, I'm dreaming.

She reopens one eye. The scorpion is in front of her. Stinger raised. It moves toward her neck. And stings her. The pain is blinding. Immediate. And without remedy. Now she knows she'll die soon. She feels her neck swell from the venom, her trachea tightening inexorably. She can barely breathe. The boys haven't come back. She no longer has the strength to scream.

It's over, she thinks. Then a sand viper slithers close. She recognizes it by the two characteristic horns. It moves slowly. Its telltale rasping sound fills the soundscape around her. It might deliver the final blow.

But at the moment of death, something strange happens. At five years old, she decides to keep her eyes wide open. And oddly enough, she's no longer afraid. An absolute calm washes over her. She rides the moon. The night is pitch black, yet the sun wraps her in its light. And with it, twelve stars.

She lets the viper do as it pleases. She knows it means her no harm. She lets it coil around her head. The cold serpentine body cools her. She just has time to see its mouth open over its venomous fangs. The viper bites her brutally on the neck. Right where the scorpion stung her. Another unbearable pain tears a silent scream from her. The blazing fire of rebirth.

It bites and doesn't let go.

I wake up with a start, face down in the gravel of the path bordering the house's yard. I'm still in the same place I was before I lost consciousness. I immediately reach for my neck—my flesh feels chewed. I can still feel the sharp pain of the sting and the bite, and right at that spot, I even think I can feel a swelling. Yet I'm still at Alexandra's, in the hills, high above Toulouse, in France. Apart from that, still dazed and with a pasty mouth, I'm alive! But completely drained of energy.

I try to let out a resonant "la!"—the "la" Franck taught me to recognize as the right note, the base note. My vocal cords vibrate, but only a hoarse sound escapes. Not the ideal "la," but not bad. I roll onto my back—the sky is clear, the stars appear in perfect sharpness, unspoiled by the city's light pollution.

So did all that really happen? Was it truly one of my childhood memories, like the others—pieces of a puzzle that has taken shape in recent months? It's the oldest by far, and strange that I never had any memory of that time before today. Or did I hallucinate after a bit of alcohol, or something else— drugs I might have unknowingly taken?

I hurt almost as if I really was stung. But obviously, I'm not dead. I couldn't have imagined all of it, could I?

Where is Lucie, whom I glimpsed in the doorway before I passed out? And Noah, my attacker? His last words come back to me, and I shiver at the memory.

What really happened? Did I dream the whole episode from the beginning?

Noah must have fled, tail between his legs—I smile painfully at that image, after the kick I gave him.

Still lying on the ground, I feel the gravel pricking my whole body. I turn my head left and right, peering into the shadowy trees. No one. Maybe the guests have started to leave. How long was I unconscious? Where's my phone? Ah, still in my back pocket. I'm too weak to get up right now, or even to roll over and grab the precious device.

Or maybe the party is at its peak, and everyone's on the other side of the house. I hear the music pounding to the rhythm of the bass through the open doors and windows. I am alive, truly alive, under the full moon that watches over me. The truth strikes me and fills me with a renewed serenity. I'm going to scream again, like the five-year-old girl who fought to live and not be left alone. I will make my voice heard and scream with all my strength, knowing that this time, someone will hear me and come for me.

MONTAUBAN, SATURDAY, JUNE 22, 2024
FINAL OF THE REGIONAL JUNIOR WOMEN'S RUGBY UNION
CHAMPIONSHIP

It started with the sensation of cold dampness down my back. The Dum Dum Girls playing in my head? Not a choice I would have made, at least not consciously. My eyes were still closed, but I could sense the light outside. I opened them. It was indeed the same grey, overcast sky. The music faded and disappeared. In its place came an indistinct blend of low and high voices all around me. Then one stood out: "Don't move. Are you okay, Nana? Can you hear me?" It was Lucie's voice—my captain. My love. Unmistakable. I couldn't see her, but she was there. Her presence was enough. I felt reassured. I opened my mouth and let out a groan that sounded something like a "yes."

A paramedic leaned over me and took over: "Can you move your head? Your hands? Your feet?" I raised a hand in response. As he went through the standard questions for someone who's lost consciousness, and as I answered automatically, I tried to catch other sounds. It seemed as though the noise in the stadium had fallen silent.

I wanted to see. I wanted to know. Suddenly, before anyone could stop me, I rolled over onto my stomach. And I saw Frédérique, frozen, bent over like a golfer, a few metres behind the ball lying on the ground before her. She was getting ready to kick the conversion, like the famous English player Dickinson. A magical moment. Time seemed to stand still. On the scoreboard in the distance, though, I could see the seconds ticking away: barely thirty seconds would remain after the restart. And our opponents would first have to recover the ball and do something with it, since the kick-off would return possession to us. Fred just had to send the ball between the uprights to add two extra points and give us the win.

She began her run-up slowly, just three steps, then sped up on the last one, swinging her leg. I heard the distinct *thunk* as her cleat struck the ball. It didn't fly as high as we'd hoped. But that didn't surprise me: Fred didn't have my mammoth kick. She knew she was a little short to take the conversion from the sideline at that distance, so instead of using energy to kick high, she went for a more direct shot, but with greater force.

From the edge of the field where I lay, I could tell the ball was heading straight for the posts. But now the kick looked too weak! The ball was descending too early to make it through! It finished its arc by bouncing off the top of the crossbar and just barely made it through the uprights.

My heart burst with joy, just as my teammates and the entire crowd erupted in cheers. Once again, the world opened up to me. I had taken one step closer to becoming who I truly am.

Dear Papa, Dear Mama, Dear Grandparents, Dear Ada and Dear Maatallah,

As-salaam-alaikum. Yes, it's really me, Fatimata! Your Nana, alive and doing better, writing to you after all this time. I know it's been a long while since you last heard from me. I have no excuse. But I can assure you that I have thought about you every single day since I left home three years ago.

Instead of trying to call or go online, I'm writing you a letter. First, because I don't yet feel ready to face you directly. I know—you might think that's cowardly. It may be. But still, a letter is something real. It doesn't disappear as soon as the call ends. It's not fleeting, or

*dependent on battery life or internet connection. You can
keep it and read it again whenever you want. It's a piece
of me I'm sending to you.*

*I truly hope this finds you in good health—especially
Grandfather and Grandmother. My escape from Atar,
away from Mohamed Ould Obeid, was something I
thought long and hard about. I'm sorry I didn't tell you
before I did it. But in my situation, it was impossible. I
hope you can understand that. I couldn't live under that
man's control any longer, even if he was a friend of
Grandfather's. And I never, ever considered ending my
own life. Call me selfish, immodest if you must. I'll
accept it. That short year I spent in his home was
terrible.*

*Instead of servitude and being cast aside, as Papa
believed I deserved after Amel's death, I chose freedom
and light. I chose life, even if it meant risking it. After
Amel died, Papa told me I should have been the one to
fall that day. That marrying Mohamed Ould Obeid was
my punishment for surviving Amel. And for me, that
marriage truly became a death sentence.*

*After I left Atar, things didn't get much better. My
journey was tragic and full of twists, yet also so similar
to that of thousands of other migrants. I lost so much
along the way, including people I held dear. People I*

couldn't have survived without. But I can't have lost
everyone. I won't believe that. I dearly hope you have
kept a place for me in your hearts.

There was also the ordeal of leaving Africa—across
deserts, on the ocean, and the Mediterranean. It was
hell. It took another year. To recover, I speak every two
weeks with a doctor, a "specialist" called a psychologist.

Still, I've learned a lot. I've grown. I've gained so much
since leaving. An education, a new family, new friends,
the chance to accomplish, as a woman, things no other
woman in our family has ever done. I don't yet know
what profession I'll pursue, but I want to go to university
and be truly useful to society. I'm no longer that skinny,
shy, dark little girl no one in the family took seriously. I
want to stand tall, even alone if I must, before the world.
I want to fight against the unjust and questionable laws
of our time. Happiness is within reach.

I promise I'll introduce you to Santiago and Marie. You
can see them in the photo I've enclosed. That's us in
front of their house. They rescued me while I was adrift
on debris from a shipwreck in the Mediterranean. I was
dying, and they gave me a second life. But you will
always be my first family. I've never forgotten you. You
don't recognize me? That's because I've gained muscle
(a lot!) and grown a bit taller. I'm no longer a child. My

body is that of a woman. Mama, I'm sure I look just like you at the same age.

Have you noticed how much better my French has gotten? I can't say the same for my Arabic—ana asif idhlk. But I'm also learning English and Spanish. In two years, I'll finish high school! This year, I was in an adaptation class with only two teachers, Marc and Jessica. It wasn't easy, but I'm about to complete the year successfully. I've also started learning piano, being able to play music makes listening to it even more joyful!

Oh, yes, one more thing: I've put all those years of running around the village to good use. I play a sport called "rugby." Maatallah, look up "rugby sevens" on your phone. Here, girls play it just as much as boys, maybe more! It's a sport where you sacrifice yourself for the team, and it's also a contact sport. Rugby has become a real passion of mine.

Papa, how's business with the tourists? I know conditions aren't ideal right now, but you're resilient, determined, and smart. I believe you'll succeed and give Mama the house of her dreams again (ha! ha!). If I can do anything to help you, at any level, I'll gladly do it. I know I've dishonoured you, and I'll do everything I can to make amends. I swear it! For me, it was literally a matter of survival.

Ada, I'm so sorry I left you behind. You must be angry, and I don't blame you. But we'll see each other again, and I'll try to earn your forgiveness however I can. You're still my little darling. Can you read and understand all of this? I didn't get a chance to tell you, but I'm giving you my secret box and all my books too. They were my most precious things. Use them well, if you haven't already. Why not dream that one day, you'll come here too?

I wish I could tell you more, give you every detail of these three years away, though never forgotten. You'll probably find this letter far too short. It's still very hard for me. But what's clearer than ever is that I love words. I love reading, and I've discovered here that I love writing, too. I've even thought about writing a book about my short life. I think it would help me—and by reading it, you could experience all the stories, thoughts, and emotions I've lived through, as if you were there. A little piece of my soul, if you will. Until then, I'll keep writing you letters.

I think of you often. If you have trouble reading some of the letters or words that are somewhat smudged here, it's because I couldn't stop a few tears from falling onto the paper. I love you.

Nana

ACKNOWLEDGMENTS

Special thanks to:

Ian Shaw at Deux Voiliers Publishing, who immediately said yes to publishing this translation.

To Emma and Dillon, my special rugby reviewers, Magali, for her ability to generate ideas continuously and to my two daughters for being who they are, and the Balima family for opening my eyes and my mind to the sub-Saharan reality.

—Didier Périès

DIDIER PÉRIÈS

Didier Périès is from Toulouse, France, and has lived in Canada since 2005. He teaches French at Ashbury College in Ottawa and at the Université du Québec en Outaouais. He is the author of the *Mystères à Natagamau* trilogy and the serialized cyberpunk novel *Le métal vaut toujours mieux que la viande*. A versatile writer, he also composes poetry and works as a newspaper columnist. For over 30 years, he has played rugby, and practiced martial arts and combat sports. Devoted to his community in Gatineau, he is politically active in defending the environment and social equity. *Fatimata* is his first novel to be translated into English. The original French text was published in spring 2025 under the title *Guelta: du Sahel au rugby.*

GLOSSARY OF FOREIGN WORDS IN THE NOVEL

Guelta: depression or basin where water has accumulated due to flooding or feeding from springs in a desert environment.

Daara: Koranic school.

Guetna: in Mauritania, festival of "desert fruits" (dates), held between mid-June and mid-August.

Inshaa Allah: literally, "If Allah wills" or "by the grace of Allah."

Melefah or *melhfa* or *boubou:* A simple piece of light fabric used to wrap around the body and hair with a set of ties.

Sarouel: baggy pants. In Mauritania, they are worn with a leather belt that hangs over the pants.

Haouli: a type of turban approximately 4 to 8 meters long that is wrapped around the head and face.

Asr: the third of the five daily prayers recommended by the Quran

Drâa or *derâa* or *boubou:* A long, loose-fitting garment, often blue or white in colour, designed to suit the climatic conditions of the desert. It is made from a lightweight fabric that protects from the sun while allowing air to circulate. Its loose fit allows for great freedom of movement.

Medh: Moorish gospel, formerly sung by slave shepherds tending their flocks, particularly by the *Haratine* people.

Haratines: a Mauri/tanian ethnic minority, descendants of Black African slaves.

Wadi: a seasonal river in North Africa or the Middle East, often dry and subject to spectacular flooding.

Batah: Sandy ground serving as the bed of a temporary wadi, or the watercourse itself.

Sufism: Sufism is an aspect of eternal, universal wisdom that became embodied in the Islamic religion, which originated in Arabia in the 7th century. It can be defined as the inner, spiritual dimension of Islam, and of Sunni Islam in particular.

Code of *Khlil:* a summary of Maliki *fiqh* rules, one of the main legal schools of Islam, influenced by Sufism.

Al-khoutba: the request for the daughter's hand in marriage by the family or representatives of the groom. This formality can take place in a small gathering or in front of an extended family gathering and allows the date of the ceremony to be set.

Al-machoura: the families of the bride and groom invite their relatives to participate in the ceremony in a consultative capacity. This stage is similar to the publication of banns in Christianity, as it allows people with important information that could prevent the marriage to come forward: this is important in a society where certain milk ties can prohibit marriage in the same way as certain blood ties.

Al-nikah: consummation of the marriage, which concludes the act and makes it effective after payment of the dowry (*mahr*) to the bride.

Pulaar: a variety of the Fulani language, found in Senegal, but also in Guinea, Gambia, Mali, and Mauritania.

Kayd: the devil's tricks, which refer to deceit, cunning, and determination.

Nazrati: Come and see

Beïdanie: The *Beïdanes, Beidanes, Beydanes,* or *Bidanes,* sometimes called White Moors, are a Moorish population found in Morocco, Mauritania, Western Sahara, Mali, Algeria, and several neighbouring countries such as Libya and Niger.

Rupestre: French for cave or rock as in "cave or rock paintings."

Hadith: Hadith are traditions relating to the deeds and words of Muhammad and his companions, which complement the Quran and form the basis of Islamic law.

Assalamu alaykum: or *Assalamu alaykum* or *As Salam alaykoum.* An Arabic greeting meaning "peace be upon you."

Ana asif idhlk: I'm sorry.

GLOSSARY OF RUGBY TERMS

Advantage: Referee allows play to continue after a foul if it benefits the non-offending team. Keeps the game flowing.

Backs: Players outside the scrum, usually faster and more agile. In 15s: scrum-half (9), fly-half (10), centres (12, 13), wings (11, 14), and fullback (15).

Bend, Touch, Set (Scrum Commands): Referee's instructions to engage the scrum.

Charge: Running directly into contact with the ball in hand.

Cleaning (Clear-out): Removing opponents from a ruck to secure the ball.

Closed Side / Open Side: The closed side is the narrow side of the field during a scrum or ruck. The open side is the wider expanse of the field.

Combination (Set Move): A rehearsed attacking play, called during a match.

Conversion Kick: After a try, worth 2 points if the ball is kicked between the posts.

Corner Try: A try scored near the touchline, making conversion more difficult.

Cross-field Kick: A tactical kick across the field to exploit space, often aimed at a winger.

Cross-field Pass: A long pass that switches play across the pitch.

Drop Kick vs. Place Kick: In the drop kick, the ball is dropped and kicked as it bounces (used for kick-offs, drop goals, conversions in 7s). In the place kick, the ball is kicked from the ground (used for penalties and conversions in 15s).

Fixing a Defender: Running at a defender to commit them, then passing to a teammate.

Fly-Half (No. 10): The team's playmaker, directing attack and usually responsible for tactical kicking.

Follow-up Kick (Chase Kick): A kick chased by the kicker or teammates to regain possession.

Forwards (The Pack): Eight players in the scrum. In the front row, there are the loosehead prop (1), hooker (2) and tighthead prop (3). In the second row are the locks (4, 5). In the back row are two flankers (6, 7) and one number eight (8)

Gap: The space between defenders, targeted by attackers.

Grounding the Ball (Scoring a Try): Applying downward pressure on the ball in the opponent's in-goal to score 5 points.

High Tackle: An illegal tackle made above the line of the shoulders, often dangerous. Penalized with a penalty, yellow card, or red card depending on severity.

Hook (Side-Step): Sudden change of direction to evade a defender.

Kick-off: Restart of play with a drop kick from halfway.

Knock-on: Losing the ball forward from hand or arm. Results in a scrum for the opposition.

Lineout: Restart after the ball goes into touch. Players line up, and the ball is thrown in between them.

Maul: When the ball carrier is held up, and teammates bind on while staying on their feet, driving forward.

Offside: Player is offside if ahead of the ball or the teammate who last played it, and interfering with play.

One-Two Pass (Give-and-Go): Passing to a teammate, running past them, and immediately receiving the ball back.

Opening (Going Wide): Passing the ball out to the backs rather than keeping play tight with the forwards.

Pass Feint (Dummy Pass): Pretending to pass to deceive a defender.

Pick and Go: Forward picks the ball from a ruck and drives forward.

Push Pass: Short, flat pass delivered at chest height with two hands.

Ruck: When the ball is on the ground and players from both teams, on their feet and bound, contest possession.

Scrum: Restart after minor infringements (e.g., knock-on). Forwards bind together and contest for the ball.

Scrum-half (No. 9): Feeds the scrum, links forwards and backs, directs play.

Skip Pass: A long pass that skips one or more teammates to reach a player further out.

Spear Tackle (Cathedral Tackle): An illegal tackle where a player lifts an opponent and drives them head- or neck-first into the ground. Considered very dangerous and usually punished with a red card.

Screw Pass (Spin Pass): Pass thrown with spin for accuracy and distance.

Try: Scored by grounding the ball in the opponent's in-goal. Worth 5 points.

Try Zone (In-Goal Area): The area behind the try line where tries are scored.

Up and Under (Garryowen)
A high, hanging kick giving chasers time to contest the ball.

PLAYLIST

CHAPTER	TITLE	ARTIST
1.	*7 seconds*	Youssou N'Dour
2.	*Birthday song*	Meklit
3.	*On ira*	Zaz
	travellers	K-Iri
4.	*Quoi de neuf*	Veemie Veezeur
	Pon de replay	Rihanna
5.	*The quiet voice*	Alexandra Stréliski
6.	*Habina*	Rachid Taha
7.	*Losing it*	Fischer
	Bad boy	Marwa Loud
8.	*Inch'Allah*	Grands corps malade
	Take it	Dom Dolla
9.	*Jammu Africa*	Ismaël Lô
10.	*No roots*	Alice Merton
	Dancing	Aaron Smith
11.	*Tengoku*	Berdzaïl
	Start me up	Rolling Stones
12.	*Wililé*	Fatoumata Diawara
13.	*Sugar*	Robin Schulz
	Homomachines	Femmouzes T.
14.	*Djon'Maja*	Victor Démé
15	*Corps étrangers*	Chantal Archambault
	Ta reine	Angèle
	You make me feel	Jimmy Somerville
16.	*Crazy in love*	Beyoncé
	Le But	Loco Locass
17.	*Yarab*	Malouma
18.	*Monnaie de singe*	Iam
	Leur dire	R'May
	Môt Cu Lua	Bich Phuong
19.	*Waidalal Waidalal*	Dimi Mint Abba
	Yar Allahoo	Dimi Mint Abba
	Ya Rayah	Rachid taha
20.	*Droit devant*	Dobacaracol

Other Titles by Deux Voiliers Publishing